Take Me
IN YOUR ARMS

JUDY LYNN HUBBARD

HARLEQUIN® KIMANI™ ROMANCE

This book is gratefully dedicated to my fabulous readers who emailed, posted on Facebook and contacted me via Twitter asking me to write a story for Cam and Angela. I sincerely hope you find their story worth the long wait. Thank you for your support, and please know that it and you mean more to me than words can say.

Recycling programs
for this product may
not exist in your area.

ISBN-13: 978-0-373-86376-1

TAKE ME IN YOUR ARMS

Copyright © 2014 by Judy Lynn Hubbard

All rights reserved. The reproduction, transmission or utilization of this work in whole or in part in any form by any electronic, mechanical or other means, now known or hereafter invented, including xerography, photocopying and recording, or in any information storage or retrieval system, is forbidden without written permission. For permission please contact Harlequin Kimani, 225 Duncan Mill Road, Toronto, Ontario M3B 3K9, Canada.

This is a work of fiction. Names, characters, places and incidents are either the product of the author's imagination or are used fictitiously, and any resemblance to actual persons, living or dead, business establishments, events or locales is entirely coincidental.

® and TM are trademarks of Harlequin Enterprises Limited or its corporate affiliates. Trademarks indicated with ® are registered in the United States Patent and Trademark Office, the Canadian Intellectual Property Office and in other countries.

For questions and comments about the quality of this book please contact us at CustomerService@Harlequin.com.

HARLEQUIN®

Printed in U.S.A.

™ www.Harlequin.com

"Can I tempt you with something?" He smiled mischievously. "I was just about to fix some lunch."

"No, thanks. I've got to get back for a staff meeting."

"Okay." He slowly walked toward her, eating up her oxygen with each step he took. "Thanks for checking on me."

"Sure."

"I'm sorry I worried you."

"I'm glad you're okay and that you're following the doctor's orders and resting." She breathed a little easier as she slipped back into her professional mode.

"I told you I would. Didn't you believe me?"

"Let's just say that I'm pleasantly surprised you are being a good boy."

"Normally, I'm not, but I have motivation to be." He ran a hand lightly down her arm before grasping her fingers. "Very lovely incentive."

"I need to leave now."

"If you must." He reluctantly released her hand. "See you tomorrow night."

If she had any sense, she'd cancel their date. Her strong reaction to his immense charm was disquieting. But she knew if she tried to back out now, he would unleash more of that charm against her until she gave in again. And frankly, she didn't think her heart could take it. Therefore, she would go on one date with him as she'd promised, but that was it.

"Bye, Cam." She turned and walked out into the hallway. He followed her to the front door, where she glanced at him and softly ordered, "Next time, answer your phone."

"I'll keep it by my side." He made an *X* over his heart with a finger—a spot her lips longed to taste. "I promise."

Books by Judy Lynn Hubbard

Harlequin Kimani Romance

These Arms of Mine
Our First Dance
Our First Kiss
Our First Embrace
Take Me In Your Arms

JUDY LYNN HUBBARD

is a Texas native who has always been an avid reader—particularly of romance. Judy loves well-written, engaging stories with characters she can identify with, empathize with and root for. When writing, she honestly can't wait to see what happens next; she knows if she feels that way, she's created characters and a story that readers will thoroughly enjoy, and that's her ultimate goal.

Dear Reader,

Finally, here is the sequel to *These Arms of Mine!* I always intended to write Cam and Angela's story immediately following Alesha and Derrick's book, but I was sidetracked by *My First Dance*. Cam and Angela wouldn't let me forget about them, though, and I'm pleased that their story is now available.

Currently, I'm working on Victor James's book (the lovable matchmaking brother from *Our First Embrace*), and I'm hoping to have his story completed soon. Follow me on my website, Facebook and/or Twitter for updates.

While I hash out some other ideas in my cluttered head, I hope you enjoy Cam and Angela's story.

As always, thanks for your support. Happy reading!

Judy

www.JudyLynnHubbard.com
Twitter: @JudyLynnHubbard
Facebook: Judy Lynn Hubbard

Chapter 1

Cameron Stewart's pupils dilated happily when his eyes focused on Angela Brown—the beautiful woman he had been thinking a lot about lately. She was standing alone across the room looking somewhat bored. He sent up a silent prayer of thanks that she appeared dateless and made his move. An assured stride carried him determinedly toward Angela, fingers grabbing a drink along the way.

They had met at Alesha and Derrick's wedding. Derrick was his best friend, and Alesha was Angela's. He'd been meaning to ask her out for quite some time; however, both of their lives had been extremely crazy for far too long, so it had never happened. They had occasionally seen each other—as they were doing now—at Alesha and Derrick's house, but that wasn't enough. He wanted to get to know her better, and he intended to make that happen right now.

At thirty-seven, he'd had his fill of dating superficial, money-hungry little girls. He wanted a real woman, and unless his keen lawyer ability to read people had deserted him, Angela fit that bill to a T. From speaking with Alesha and from his own observations, he knew Angela was an accomplished nurse who was dedicated to her career. She was also a wonderful friend and a genuinely nice lady who cared about people. She was just what the doctor ordered, and he intended to happily take his medicine like a good little boy.

"Why, Angela Brown, I didn't expect to see you here tonight, but I'm glad I did." At his statement, Angela turned from the appetizer tray to face him. "Hello."

"Hi, Cam." Angela smiled, and what a beautiful smile it was. "How are you?"

"Much better now that I'm seeing you again."

"Flatterer." Her smile brightened, nearly knocking his socks off.

"Just stating a fact, ma'am." Eyes slowly drifted over her from head to toe. Lord, she was wearing the hell out of her sleeveless little black dress. "You look beautiful tonight."

"Thanks." She eyed his designer navy suit and returned his compliment, "You look good, too."

"Having a good time?" At his question, she glanced around the room and shrugged.

"Not really. This isn't exactly my cup of tea." At his questioning expression, she elaborated, "Alesha pleaded with me to come. She wanted to have at least one friend to seek refuge with once Derrick started talking politics."

"Oh, I see." Cam laughed. "I'm glad she browbeat you into coming."

A smile played about her full lips. "And why is that?"

"Because I've been thinking about you lately—a lot."

"You have?" A perfectly arched brow rose in surprise. "Why?"

"What do you mean, why?"

"I think that's a fair question." She chuckled. "We haven't seen each other in quite some time."

"*That's* why I've been thinking about you." Cam grinned and added, "It's way past time we had a bona fide date. So what do you say, gorgeous?" He treated her to a smile designed to melt any resistance. "Will you go out with me?"

"We've gone out before, Cam," Angela reminded him, sipping her tonic and lime. "About six months ago, if memory serves."

"With Alesha and Derrick in tow." His distasteful expression elicited a soft laugh from her. "I'm talking about you and me." He paused for emphasis and stressed, "Alone."

"We're alone right now." A well-manicured hand indicated the secluded corner of the crowded room they occupied. "Aren't we?"

"This doesn't count."

"Why not?" Angela placed a hand on a shapely hip, inviting his eyes to feast on her perfect curves.

"Because we didn't come together and—" Cam glanced around the room until his eyes locked on their hosts across the room "—because our best friends are hovering around in the background watching us, even though they're pretending not to."

Angela followed his gaze to where Alesha and Derrick stood, covertly glancing at them from time to time. She laughed and drawled, "They do seem interested in us, don't they?"

"Mmm-hmm." Cam nodded and grinned. "I can practically see the matchmaking wheels turning in their heads."

Angela suddenly frowned. "I hope not."

Cam's eyes refocused on her. "Is the thought of being set up with me so distasteful?"

"I didn't mean it like that," she said quickly. "Any woman would consider herself lucky to go out with you."

"Thanks." Cam smiled, took a step closer and smoothly

replied, "I'm not interested in any woman, though. I only want to go out with you."

"Cam, you don't know anything about me," she said softly.

"That's what I'm *trying* to remedy." He winked, and a smile played about her tempting lips.

"I'll bet you were a handful growing up."

"That's what my mom says," he admitted with a grin. "Dance with me."

"There's no music," she informed him, and his grin widened.

Please, like I'd let a little detail like that dissuade me. "I'll sing."

She arched an eyebrow. "Can you sing?"

"I can carry a tune," he promised, placing a hand on her waist. "Care to try me?"

His eyes zeroed in on the rapidly beating pulse in her neck, and he smiled. Good, he did affect her. For a moment, he thought she was going to take him up on his offer, but then she shook her head and stepped back. He reluctantly allowed his hand to drop to his side.

"Maybe another time," she responded a little breathlessly.

"I'll hold you to that," he promised. "So how about it?"

She blinked. "How about what?"

"Go out with me," Cam reiterated his previous request.

"I don't think so."

"Don't you think it's about time we see if this spark between us will flame?" He heard, saw and felt her quickly indrawn breath at his suggestive statement.

"Speaking of the time, I think I've done my duty for tonight." She skillfully avoided answering his question. "If you'll excuse me, I'm going to say good-night to Derrick and Alesha. I have to be at the hospital very early tomorrow."

"May I take you home?"

"No, thanks, I have my car."

"That's a pity." He sighed heavily, and she smiled.

"Sorry."

"It's okay." He took a step closer, watching her gorgeous eyes constrict at his proximity. "But just so you know, I'm not giving up until you agree to go out with me, Angela."

"No." A smile played about her mauve-colored lips that begged to be kissed. "I'm sure you won't."

"Do you want me to?" He studied her carefully as she mulled over his question—a question that really wasn't a difficult one to answer. Her hesitation both intrigued him and gave him hope. "Well?"

"I like you, Cam," she slowly admitted. "But I'm afraid my plate is entirely too full right now to add anything else to it."

"But you still have to eat." His eyes slowly raked over her, and his hands longed to do the same. "Don't you?"

Confusion lit up her expressive eyes as if she didn't know exactly how to respond to his question. Good, he had her off balance. Taking advantage of that fact, he moved in closer and trailed a finger down her bare arm, watching her closely the entire time. He felt the shiver that ran through her, heard the soft gasp that escaped from her slightly parted lips and witnessed the noticeable darkening of her brown eyes. She wasn't as indifferent as she would have him believe.

There was definitely something between them, and the time was finally ripe to explore it. He hadn't aggressively pursued her when they first met a year ago because frankly he hadn't had the time to devote to wooing her the way she deserved. However, that wasn't the case anymore. His commitment to Derrick's senatorial campaign was fulfilled, and his successful law firm was sailing along smoothly, which left him free to cultivate his personal life—and he was itching to see if Angela Brown would be a good fit in said personal life.

"I…" Angela shook her head as if to clear it and took a step away from him. "It was good seeing you again." Her voice was breathless and made his skin tingle with excitement.

"You, too." He grasped her hand, almost groaning at the feel of her soft skin against his, and brought it to his lips. "I look forward to our next encounter, which will be soon, if I have my way."

She tilted her head to the side, studying him as if she was trying to figure out what to do with him. He had a few ideas he would love to share with her. The thought coerced a wicked grin from him.

"Good night, Cam." She arched an eyebrow when his grip tightened on her hand before reluctantly releasing it.

"Good night." He smiled and watched her walk across the room, then say a few words to Derrick and Alesha before heading for the door. She paused, seemed to wage a silent battle and then turned and stared at him. Everything stopped as their eyes met and held for a few electric seconds that seemed like hours. Then she broke eye contact and walked out of the room, taking the light with her.

She was like a breath of fresh air, and he had been deprived of oxygen for far too long. His smile widened, and he rubbed a hand across his bald head before scratching his hair-covered chin. What a beautiful, intriguing woman Angela Brown was. He felt more alive than he had in a long time after being in her presence, and he couldn't wait until he saw her again.

He felt ridiculously happy and almost giddy from their impromptu meeting, which had him planning his next move. He grinned widely. Oh yeah, it was definitely on.

Cam shifted the gears of his apple-red Corvette as the car ate up the road. His fingers lovingly caressed the leather-covered steering wheel. He adored this car and found himself wishing he was on the open road so that he could really let her go. However, cognizant of the fact that he was traveling through city streets, he reduced his speed to acceptable levels before coming to a halt at a red light.

He couldn't wait to get to George Washington University Hospital. There was a gorgeous nurse there with whom he had special business. He grinned as he thought of Angela. She'd be surprised to see him, but he had meant what he said to her a few nights ago—now that the craziness in both their lives had settled down, he had every intention of getting to know her better because he felt alive in her presence, and he was now convinced that she felt the strong attraction between them, too.

He planned on persuading her to have dinner with him—even if it was just cafeteria food. He had done some checking and knew she was on duty tonight, and unable to suppress the need to see her right now, here he was, prepared to make the ultimate sacrifice and eat hospital food if it meant he could spend some time with her.

Wow, he really did like her.

He chuckled as the light turned green and his foot depressed the accelerator. He had barely moved when out of the corner of his left eye, he saw a black blur speeding toward him. Turning his head, his eyes widened as a car barreled through the red light.

"I'll be—"

He tried to maneuver out of the vehicle's destructive path but was unsuccessful as it collided with his, side-swiping him. He cursed while turning the wheel, trying to right his suddenly out-of-control car.

The entire accident only took seconds that stretched out like interminable minutes. The sounds of crunching, grinding twisted metal, tires screeching, and exploding glass filled his ears as his car went into a tailspin. He frantically tried to control the spinning vehicle, but despite his best efforts, it hit something hard; the airbag deployed, blocking his vision, and then blackness enveloped him.

Angela Brown walked through the busy halls of George Washington University Hospital toward the emergency room feeling right at home. If there was one place she loved more than the operating room, it was the E.R. with its continuous beehive of activity. She absently ran fingers through her short dark brown, almost black, hair before checking the pockets of her baby-blue scrubs for her watch, which she found and placed on her right wrist. She was on her way to lead the triage team and had no sooner made it into the treatment area when EMS personnel wheeled in a gurney upon which lay an immobile man dressed in an expensive designer suit, whose face was obscured by an oxygen mask.

"What's the story?" Angela studied the papers handed to her while the other team members transferred the man to the treatment table.

"Motor vehicle collision," one of the EMS workers answered. "Restrained driver. Airbag deployed."

"Vitals?"

"Stable."

"How long has he been unconscious?"

"A few minutes maybe—since we arrived at the scene. Looks like he hit the steering wheel or the dashboard pretty hard."

"So you couldn't get a history from him."

"Nope."

Angela nodded before turning her attention to her staff. "Is Dr. Donnelly on the way?" At the nod from one of the nurses, she said, "Let's get started on routine labs and exam, Sheila. I'm sure Dr. Donnelly will order a CT head, spine series, chest X-ray and abdominal series."

"Will do."

Angela helped Sheila remove the patient's designer suit jacket before she pulled his oxygen mask off and let out a shocked gasp. Cam Stewart! It couldn't be, but it was. She'd know that handsome face anywhere—especially since it had only been a couple of days since she had last seen him.

"Angela?" Sheila touched her arm. "Are you all right?"

"What?" She tore her eyes away from Cam's unusually impassive face to stare into her friend's questioning gaze. "Yes, I'm fine."

"Do you know him?"

"Yes."

"Maybe you should let someone else—"

"No!" The single word was spoken more forcefully than she intended. Taking a deep breath and releasing it, she said, "I'm fine, Sheila."

"If you two are involved—"

"We're not. He's the best friend of Alesha's husband," Angela further explained, referencing their former co-worker.

"Oh, I see." Sheila nodded, satisfied with her explanation. "Well, let's take good care of him, then."

"Absolutely," Angela agreed. She needed to call Ale-

sha and Derrick, but first things first. She snapped back
into emergency mode and did her job, saying a silent
prayer hoping Cam would be all right.

"Let me take him and put him down, babe." Alesha's
hand gravitated toward the sleeping two-month-old son
nestled in Derrick's arms.

"In a minute." Derrick gazed lovingly at the little boy.
"I haven't seen him all day."

Alesha smiled tolerantly. "You are spoiling him."

Derrick glanced up and grinned. "Like you're not."

"It doesn't matter what I do because you're bad enough
for both of us," Alesha reasoned. "When you're gone, D.J.
just wants to be held and held all day long."

"And you're only too happy to oblige, aren't you?" He
chuckled as she softly touched D.J.'s cheek.

Before she could answer, the phone rang. She reached
over to pick it up. "Hello."

"Alesha, it's Angela."

"Hi, Angie." Alesha tucked her legs underneath her.
"What's up?"

"I want you to remain calm." At Angela's words, the
hair on the back of Alesha's neck stood up.

"I was calm until you said that." Alesha sat up a little
straighter. "What's going on?"

"What's wrong?" Derrick glanced at her, and she
shrugged.

"I don't want you and Derrick to worry," Angela began.
"He's stable, and I'm sure he's going to be fine."

"Who's going to be fine, Angie?"

"Cam, he was in a car accident."

"Cam?" Alesha's worried eyes found Derrick, who
immediately tensed at the mention of his best friend.
"How bad?"

"What's happened to Cam?" Derrick asked. Alesha could feel the apprehension rolling off her husband.

"Just a minute, babe." Alesha touched his cheek reassuringly and continued talking to Angela. "How long has he been there?"

"Not long. He was brought into the E.R. by EMS about an hour and a half ago. I was part of the team working on him. He's unconscious." Angela seemed reluctant to admit this, and then hurriedly added, "But his vitals are strong and stable."

"We'll be right down, Angie. Thanks for calling." Alesha hung up the phone without waiting for a response. "Cam was in a car accident. Angie says he's stable…but unconscious."

"Damn," Derrick swore softly and stood.

"Let me take D.J. upstairs, and then we can head out." She took their still-sleeping son from his arms.

"You don't have to come with me."

"Of course I do. Cam is family." She kissed him softly. "He'll be all right, babe," she promised before heading for the stairs. "If you leave without me, I'll have your head."

"I won't." He managed a slight smile. "Hurry."

"I'll just tell Emma we're going and be right back," she said, referring to their housekeeper as she hurried up the stairs.

"Jeez," Cam groaned, eyes closed. "Why does my head hurt so much?"

"You have a concussion." Angela's fingers touched his badly bruised temple gently. His eyes sprang open at the sound of her voice, and his frowning eyes focused on her.

"Angela?"

"In the flesh." She smiled, relieved he recognized her.

"Where am I?" He glanced around the stark white room before returning his confused eyes to her.

"In the hospital." She took out a penlight and shone it into each of his eyes.

"What happened?" He shooed the annoying light away from his eyes. "How did I get a concussion?"

She studied him closely. "Don't you remember?"

Cam seemed to think for a few minutes before responding, "Some idiot ran a red light and plowed right into me."

"That's right." She glanced at the monitors over his bed to check his vitals, which thankfully were normal.

"Oh, my poor baby," Cam groaned in misery. "She's totaled. I know it."

Angela chuckled at his obvious angst. He looked so comically forlorn over an inanimate object that she couldn't stop herself from laughing.

"I would think you'd be more concerned with your own welfare instead of your car's."

"I'm fine." He pressed a button to raise the head of the bed into a sitting position. "But my poor Yvette." He dramatically brought both hands to his bald head. "She's toast."

Angela tilted her head thoughtfully and asked, "Why do men insist on referring to their vehicles as female?"

His frown quickly turned into a wicked smile. "Are you sure you want to know?"

"Of course." She wanted to keep him talking to make sure he had all his faculties about him.

"Okay." His smile widened. "On the perfect car, like a good woman, the first thing we notice is the body—the sleek, appealing curves and pleasing aesthetics. If those attributes grab and hold our attention, we can't wait to see what's on the inside to make sure she's not just another pretty face. We check under the hood to see if her engine and inner workings are powerful, well tuned and, more importantly, turn us on. If they do, we have to step inside and sit down to ascertain if her soft curves will cradle us in all the right places—maddeningly caressing us every second we're inside her, making us feel right at home." Angela's breathing was arrested, and she was certain her pupils dilated, judging by Cam's sexy grin before he continued, "If she's the right one, she's responsive to our every whim, caress and desire. She heightens all of our senses and gives us the ride of our lives until we can't wait to get back inside of her again and again."

Angela was breathing hard when his soft, sexy voice finally ended the most erotic description of a car she had ever heard. Mercy, she needed a cold glass of water.

"I see." She purposefully averted her eyes on the pretense of removing the blood pressure cuff from his muscled upper arm.

"You asked." Cam's voice held a hint of laughter.

"I did." She turned away from his intense gaze to pour him some water.

"Are you all right?"

She took a moment to compose herself before turning around to face him again. "The question is, are you all right?" Thankfully, she sounded coolly professional when she felt anything but.

"I told you, I'm good." She agreed he certainly was good enough to tease her. "How long have I been here?"

She glanced at her watch. "A few hours. Here, drink this." He took the glass and downed the contents before returning it to her. "More?"

"No, thanks." A smile turned up the corners of his mouth. "You know, when the accident happened, I was on my way to see you."

"You were?" Her eyes widened in shock. "Why?"

"I was going to ask you to dinner."

"Why?"

"Why?" He echoed, laughed and answered, "Because I want to spend time with you." He scratched his hair-covered chin thoughtfully with his free hand and said, "We should have gotten together last year."

"Things happen for a reason." Angela shrugged. "You were busy with Derrick's campaign. I was *very* busy with my new promotion to head nurse, and—"

"All true," he interrupted, his thumb caressing the back of her hand. "What about now?"

"What about now?" Lord, she wished he would stop stroking her fingers with his. It felt too good. What was it about this man that sent her pulse racing?

"Is the time right for us to get to know each other better now?" At her silence he continued. "I meant what I said a few nights ago. I really want to get to know you better. Don't you want that, too?"

"Cam, this isn't the time or the place for this." She tried to retrieve her hand, which he refused to release. "I meant what I said, too. I really don't have time…"

Thankfully, Derrick and Alesha chose that moment to enter the room, allowing Angela the diversion she needed to retrieve her hand and move to the foot of the bed out of Cam's physical reach, though his eyes stared straight through her, silently promising they weren't finished with their conversation.

Derrick walked over and squeezed Cam's shoulder. "Thank God, you're awake."

"Don't tell me you were worried about me." Cam smiled at his best friend.

"We both were." Alesha squeezed his hand. "How do you feel?"

"I'm fine." He gingerly touched his temple. "Just a few aches."

"Consider yourself lucky." Derrick heaved a sigh of relief.

"I do." Cam grinned at Angela and then glanced around the room as if searching for something. He returned his attention to Angela and asked, "Hey, where are my clothes?"

Angela frowned. "Why?"

"That's your favorite word, isn't it?" At her frown he elaborated. "I want to get dressed. I can't wear this thing home." Cam pointed to the flimsy hospital gown. "Since Derrick is here, he can give me a ride."

"You're not going anywhere, Cameron Stewart," Angela firmly promised.

"Oh, yes, I am."

"Oh, no, you're not." Angela placed her hands on her hips, preparing for a battle she was determined to win. "Not until you're officially released."

"Says who?" Cam defiantly crossed his arms across his chest. "You're not the boss of me."

"Maybe she isn't," Derrick said, chuckling, "but I know who is."

Cam turned his frowning gaze to his friend. "What does that mean?"

Derrick took his phone out of his pocket. "Do you really want me to make this call?" Comprehension dawned in Cam's eyes.

"You wouldn't."

"Oh, wouldn't I?" Derrick turned his phone so Cam could clearly see the name and number on the screen. "Are you staying, or do I press Dial?"

Alesha and Angela stared at each other in confusion and then glanced from Derrick to Cam. Cam glared at

Derrick for long, tense seconds, but Derrick didn't flinch. Finally Cam sighed in resignation, all fight seeming to leave him.

"All right, you blackmailer." Cam dejectedly plopped back against the pillows. "I'll stay."

"Wise choice," Derrick said.

"Who were you going to call?" Alesha asked.

"His mother." Derrick laughed at Cam's dark scowl.

"Oh." Alesha said, "Shouldn't we call her anyway?"

"No, I'm fine," Cam quickly interjected. "If you call her, she'll drop everything, hop on a plane and mother me to death for the next few weeks. I don't have the strength for that. I was just in a car accident." His loud sigh elicited laughter from all present. Cam fixated on Derrick's pleased countenance. "I'll pay you back for this, Senator, when I get out of here."

"I'll be ready for you." Derrick winked. "You really should call Mama Mabel, though."

"I know, and I will when I'm home and I can assure her that I'm fine."

"Okay," Derrick reluctantly agreed. "Since you're obviously in good hands and apparently as stubborn as ever, Alesha and I will leave you alone. We just had to make sure you were all right."

"Thanks for coming by to coerce me into staying."

"Anytime." Derrick patted his shoulder.

"Obey your doctors, and you'll get out of here soon." Alesha bent down and kissed his cheek.

"I'll try." He gave her a halfhearted smile.

"Do you need anything?" Derrick asked.

"No." Cam's eyes strayed to Angela. "I have everything I need."

"I see." Derrick smiled, following his friend's line of vision. "Okay, then. We'll check on you tomorrow."

"I guess I'll be here," Cam said grudgingly, watching Derrick and Alesha leave hand in hand.

"You'll be here," Angela said, and smiled when he groaned as if in pain. When he eyed the closet, she warned, "Don't even think about it."

"Think about what?" he asked innocently.

"Leaving," Angela answered. "If you're not here when I come back to check on you, I'm going to call Derrick and tell him to call your mother."

Angela fought a smile. Cam sighed heavily and looked like a child caught with his hand in the cookie jar. He really was extremely cute.

"I'll be here," he promised before adding, "I'm really enjoying the company of my beautiful nurse."

"Get some rest." Angela ignored his second comment. "I'll check on you later."

"I'll look forward to it."

Angela shook her head at his wolfish grin and exited the room. A smile turned up the corners of her mouth, and she chuckled lightly as she walked down the hall. Cameron Stewart was something else. He was just as handsome and funny as ever.

If she wasn't a magnet for disaster when it came to relationships, she would have taken the time to get to know him better. However, she knew from past experience that she didn't do relationships well at all, and she had no intention of getting serious with anyone ever again.

She was focused on her career like a laser beam, and that's where her attention would remain. But…if she was going to date someone, Cameron Stewart would be at the top of the list, she admitted.

"But you're not looking for a relationship," she firmly reminded herself. "No good will come from that, and you know it."

Having sufficiently chastised herself, she quickly walked down the hall, away from the heady temptation that was Cameron Stewart.

Chapter 2

The next morning when Angela entered Cam's room, he was sitting up in bed flipping through channels on the television. His frowning countenance and cagey appearance informed her he couldn't wait to escape from what he deemed his unjust imprisonment. She had the feeling that if he wasn't released soon, he'd plan on leaving against medical advice. Luckily for all concerned, his test results had come back negative, and she had the feeling he'd be released today.

"Good morning," she greeted him brightly. "How are you feeling?"

"Bored out of my mind." Cam threw the remote back onto the bed. "When can I get outta here?"

"Tired of us already?"

"Of you? Never." His appreciative eyes roamed over her face. "Of this place? Definitely. I don't do hospitals."

"Well, you'll do this one until your doctor says otherwise."

"I feel fine." She fought a smile at his defiant expression. "Why can't I leave now?"

"Dr. Jackson wants to make sure you're okay. You don't want to go home only to be readmitted, do you?"

He shuddered at her question. "Heaven forbid."

"Well then, be a good boy, behave and just enjoy the rest."

"Rest?" He raised an eyebrow, and the corners of his mouth turned down. "You're kidding, right?"

"What do you mean by that?"

"People come in here at all hours of the night, poking, prodding and taking blood, needing to check this or that and asking if I'm okay, or more annoyingly, waking me up when I do manage to catch a few z's to see how I'm doing." He paused for emphasis before ending theatrically. "Who can rest in this place?"

Light laughter bubbled from Angela's smiling lips as he finished his heartfelt tirade. "Would you rather they ignored you and missed something vital that was detrimental to your health?" she asked.

Cam cracked a smile. "Taking their side against me, huh?"

"I'm part of *them*," she reminded him wryly.

"*You* can bother me all night long anytime you want." Cam's eyes sparkled. "In fact, I wish you would."

"Do you now?"

"Mmm-hmm." He treated her to a disarming smile and asked, "Will you go out with me when I'm sprung from this joint?"

"No." She bit her lip to stop a smile when he frowned at her quick denial.

"Why not?"

"Maybe I'm just not interested in you romantically."

"Oh, you're interested," he replied confidently, and grinned when she chuckled.

"What a conceited thing to say."

"It's not conceit," he quickly denied. "I know you feel that spark of awareness between us whenever we're in close proximity." Oh yeah, she felt it, but she had no intention of acting on it.

"Sorry to disappoint you, but no, I haven't." She told

the little white lie with a straight face, hoping to convince him of her sincerity.

"No?" His eyes twinkled in challenge.

"No." Before she could blink, he grabbed her hand and pulled her until she was sitting beside him on the bed. "Let go, Cam."

"What's wrong?" He tugged on her hand until she was leaning over him slightly. "Tempted?"

"No," she lied. *Who wouldn't be tempted by your gorgeous brown eyes, alive with mirth and dogged determination?* "Not in the least."

His free hand moved to softly caress her jaw before anchoring behind her neck. "Then why are you trembling?"

"You're imagining things." Lord, he was too close, too handsome and much too tempting.

"Am I?" He pulled her nearer still. "I don't think I am."

"Cam, please..." She placed her free hand on his chest for leverage, which was a big mistake because the feel of his hard muscles only made her want to press tight against his unbending length instead of escaping.

"Please what? Kiss you?" She fought a groan when his gaze darted to her lips before returning to her turbulent eyes. "You don't have to worry. I plan on kissing you a lot once I get out of here. In fact, let's get in a few trial runs. Shall we?"

At that moment the door opened and Derrick waltzed in. He chuckled when he saw Cam and Angela's intimate position. Angela was relieved—and if she was honest, a little disappointed—by the intrusion.

"I see you're feeling *much* better," Derrick drawled, placing a change of clothes over the back of a chair.

Cam sighed. "Senator, you have lousy timing."

"Sorry. Want me to leave?"

"No." Angela seized the opportunity to break free of Cam's loosened hold and back away toward the door. "Good morning, Derrick."

"Angela." Derrick grinned.

"We'll finish this later, Angela," Cam promised from the bed.

"The only thing you're going to finish is your breakfast." Her shaky voice took the sting out of that order as she pointed to his tray. "See you later, Derrick," she murmured, and left.

"Well, well, well." Derrick eyed his friend with interest.

Cam folded his arms behind his head and reclined on the pillows. "What are you grinning about?"

"Are you finally ready to date Angela?" Derrick asked.

"Yes," Cam affirmed. "You know I believe in taking advantage of opportunity, and Lord knows there's nothing like a brush with danger to light a fire of urgency underneath you."

"So—" Derrick pulled a chair to the bedside and sat down "—am I to understand that now you're happy about your accident even though your baby was totaled?"

"Oh, please, don't remind me about that," Cam groaned at the mention of his beloved car. "It's going to take a long time to get over losing Yvette." He paused and then said philosophically, "I guess you have to lose something to gain something, though."

"True." Derrick stretched his legs out in front of him and switched subjects. "Have you called Mama Mabel yet?"

"I'll call her when I get home, dude." Cam sighed and treated him to a frustrated glare. "When I get home."

"She's gonna skin you alive for not calling her sooner."

"Not really." Cam smiled slyly. "I'll just tell her I was out of it and thought *you* had called her." Alarm lit up Derrick's eyes, and Cam's smile widened.

Derrick sat up straight in his chair and growled, "Oh, no, you don't!"

"Look at you, scared of my mama!" Cam slapped his thigh and laughed heartily.

Derrick smiled and asked, "And you're not?"

Cam sobered and said, "I plead the Fifth."

"You just keep me out of your alibi."

"I'll consider it, although it would be the perfect payback for your blackmail to keep me here last night."

"Cameron—" Derrick's eyes glinted dangerously "—you wouldn't want me to tell Angela some of your most embarrassing moments, would you?"

"No more than you'd want me to share a few of yours with Alesha," Cam shot back easily. At Derrick's darkening countenance, he promised, "Don't worry. I know how to handle my mother without implicating you."

"Good," Derrick said, relaxing back in his chair again. "Do you know when they're going to spring you yet?"

"Today, I hope." Cam frowned at his untouched breakfast tray. "I can't take any more of this so-called food."

"You'll live."

"Easy for you to say."

Cam's eyes suddenly turned to the door through which Angela had escaped. The delighted expression spread across his face until he laughed out loud again. Cam's jubilance coaxed a corresponding smile out of Derrick.

"What's so funny?"

"I have the feeling totaling my car is going to be well worth it in the long run. It's given me a new lease on life."

"Uh-oh."

"Uh-oh is right," Cam agreed. "I'm about to unleash

the full brunt of my charm on Angela Brown, and you, my brother, know how devastatingly charming I can be."

He winked at Derrick, who shook his head and wagged a finger in reproof before joining in his friend's optimistic, determined laughter.

Later that morning when Angela entered Cam's room, she found him fully dressed in faded jeans and a white T-shirt that was stretched tight across his muscled chest. He was standing by the bed and talking on his phone. He motioned for her to come in and quickly ended his call.

"I see you got the word from Dr. Jackson that you're being released."

"Not a moment too soon." Cam raised his eyes heavenward. "I told you I was fine."

Lord, yes, you are! she couldn't help silently agreeing.

"Well, it's our job to make sure. Now that everything officially checks out, we agree with you." She paused before adding, "You were very lucky."

"In more ways than one." Her breath caught at the way he was looking at her. "Cam…"

"What?"

He didn't try to mask the appreciation shining in his eyes as he slowly examined her from head to toe and back again. She'd never met a man who made her feel like the sexiest woman he had ever seen when she was dressed in loose-fitting, bland hospital scrubs—until now. A shiny stethoscope was slung around her neck, and Cam had a look in his eyes like he would love to play doctor with her, and if she was honest, that might be a lot of fun.

"Nothing," she finally answered, shaking her head to chase away forbidden thoughts. There were a lot of things she could have said, but she settled on, "I just wanted to say goodbye and take care."

"Oh, this isn't goodbye," he said, walking toward her.

"You are leaving today, aren't you?"

"With wings." He stopped directly in front of her. At five feet eleven inches, she had to tilt her head to stare into his eyes, which made him a little over six feet.

"Well then, this is goodbye."

"This is only *see you later,*" he contradicted. "And speaking of later, I have a request of you."

"What?" She eyed him warily.

"Have dinner with me tonight."

"I'm working tonight."

"Tomorrow night, then."

"I don't think so."

He frowned. "Why not?"

"Because you need rest." She adopted her sternest voice and continued, "You suffered a mild concussion, and you should be concentrating on your recovery, not dating."

"I'll rest for the remainder of the day and tonight, *if* you'll have dinner with me tomorrow night," he bargained. "Come on." He grinned infectiously. Lord, she could make out faint dimples visible through the light hair covering his cheeks, as if he needed another attribute to add to his handsomeness. "Give me a reward for being a model patient."

She arched an eyebrow. "You think you've been a model patient?" He nodded vigorously, and she suppressed a smile with difficulty. "I think your head injury was worse than we thought."

"I don't know what you're smirking about. I've been very agreeable." At her continued skeptical expression, he suggested, "Ask any of my nurses."

"That won't be necessary. I'll let you cling to your delusions."

"Will you also reward my good behavior and go out with me tomorrow night?" he persisted.

"Isn't getting out of here incentive enough for you?"

"You've got me there," he quickly agreed. "But..."

She sighed. "There's always a *but*."

"Yes there is," he agreed. "And this one's very important."

"Well, let's hear it," she prompted drily.

"*But* we've waited long enough to go out on a real date. Granted, we've both been insanely busy, *but* now fate has brought us back together, so let's not waste this opportunity. Let's seize the moment and do something we should have done months ago."

"Is that the reason you want to go out with me? To check off some *to-do* list?" she challenged.

"Of course it isn't."

"Why *do you* want to go out with me?"

"Because I like you. I have since the moment I met you," he answered immediately. His warm eyes held hers captive. "Don't you like me?"

"You're a very nice man, Cam, but—"

"No buts," he interrupted with a smile.

"No fair, you got to use buts, so I should too," she argued.

"Sorry." He shrugged. "Those are the rules."

"Some rules," she huffed.

"Come on. You know you want to give in. I promise to show you the time of your life if you'll go out with me." A smile played about her lips at his persistence. "I'm not seeing anyone. Are you?"

"No." Her truthful response tumbled out before she could stop it.

"I don't understand how that's possible, but I'm not looking a gift horse in the mouth." He grinned again, showing off those dimples that her fingers were itching to trace. "Don't you want to see where this leads—finally?"

She did and she didn't. She did like Cam, she had since meeting him, but she was dedicated to her career—a career that was very demanding of her time and focus. She also had a lousy track record with men, and she didn't want to travel down that losing road again…but maybe this time could be different. Maybe Cam would be different. He certainly made her feel different. She wished she knew whether that was good or bad.

"You're thinking too much," he said. "That means you really want to say yes."

"It means no such thing."

"Yes, it does." He reached out and took her hand. "Come on, Angela, you know we're long overdue for our date."

"We've seen each other several times. A few nights ago, to be exact," she reminded him.

"For a few minutes at Alesha and Derrick's." He grimaced, and she bit back a laugh with difficulty. "That hardly qualifies as a date. Does it?"

"That depends on your perspective."

"Well, my perspective is that seeing each other at our mutual friends' house is not a real date." He made another distasteful face, and this time she did laugh. "Come on, I'll show you the time of your life." Of that she had absolutely no doubt. She was having a good time just standing here sparring with him.

She hadn't been on a real date in ages—years, in fact, and with good reason. She liked her life the way it was—predictable and uncomplicated. She had no intention of starting anything serious with anyone, but where was the harm in sharing a good meal with a man who was funny, smart and godfather to their best friends' son while she was the godmother?

"All right," she heard herself agreeing.

"Excellent." He brought the back of her hand to his lips, sending goose bumps up her arm. Suddenly the room seemed much too small for the two of them, especially when he said, "Your skin is very soft."

"Um…I have to go." She cursed her breathless voice and removed her hand from his. "I'm due in the O.R."

"Okay, I guess I can't object to that." Her eyes widened when his fingers smoothed her bangs off her eyebrows. "I'm looking forward to our date, Angela."

"Just remember you promised me a great time." She was surprised she could articulate this, because his nearness was doing strange things to her ability to breathe naturally.

"And I'll deliver," he promised. "Where would you like to go?"

"Surprise me."

"You may be sorry you said that," he teased.

"On second thought…"

He placed a silencing finger lightly on her lips. "Too late to take it back." Her lips tingled from his touch. She took a step backward, ending the disturbing contact.

"Your nurse will be in with your discharge papers soon."

"Hallelujah!" A small smile played about her lips at his jubilant response.

"Try to contain your enthusiasm."

"No can do." His smile widened. "I can't wait to get outta here."

"Just make sure you rest when you get home."

"I will." He paused before pointedly reminding her, "You've given me great incentive to. I'll pick you up tomorrow at seven?" he asked as she backed away toward the door.

"That'll be fine."

"I can't wait." He stepped forward and touched her cheek. "See you tomorrow night."

"Tomorrow," she echoed before leaving.

On the other side of the door, she took and released a deep breath. What had she gotten herself into? It was just one date with an acquaintance—nothing serious, and she would take great care to make sure to keep it that way. Casual and uncomplicated. That was her plan, that was her goal, and she would stick to it no matter how charming Cameron Stewart was. And Lord knows he was the very definition of charming!

Angela walked into her office and sank gratefully into her comfortable chair behind her paper-laden desk. Closing tired eyes, she sighed audibly. She was beat but still had a lot of hours left before she could go home. She groaned as that horrible realization hit her. At least she had time for a decent lunch before her evening staff meeting.

Opening her eyes, she picked up numerous pink message slips with a weary hand and began reading each one. Boy, was she popular today. One message in particular caught her eye—it was from Cam. She checked the time and found he had called an hour ago. She wondered what he wanted. Maybe he had a question about his discharge instructions. Well, there was only one way to find out.

Picking up the phone, she dialed the number and waited for him to answer. He didn't. She hung up and redialed, thinking she must have pressed a wrong digit somewhere. Again, there was no response. She bolted upright in her chair, fingers tightening on the receiver as she waited for him to answer. When he didn't, she tried to calm her suddenly racing heart.

Why wasn't he answering his phone? Why had he called her? Was it for an innocent reason? Like he simply wanted to tell her where they were going for dinner tomorrow? Or had he been feeling ill and needed some medical advice?

"Get a grip, Angela," she sternly admonished. "He wouldn't have been released if he wasn't okay." She frantically dialed his number again with the same results—no answer. "Calm down. He's fine," she said, trying to reassure herself.

She considered ringing Derrick or Alesha and asking them to check on him but quickly dismissed that idea. She didn't want to upset them unnecessarily, and such a call from her would do just that. Besides, she was upset enough for all of them.

Without success, she fought valiantly to keep dire thoughts from racing through her mind. What if Cam had passed out and couldn't answer the phone? What if he was…? She glanced at her watch. She had about two-and-a-half hours before her meeting; that should be enough time. She could get his address from his hospital chart.

Coming to a decision, she stood, grabbed her purse from the desk drawer and hurried out.

Chapter 3

Angela drove down George Washington Memorial Parkway for about forty-five minutes until she reached the high-class neighborhood of Potomac, Maryland, where Cam lived. She admired the beautiful multimillion-dollar mansions that sat an aesthetically good distance from the road, until she located Cam's house—a sprawling two-story white edifice surrounded by a white iron security fence, which thankfully was open. As she drove up to the house, she spared a quick glance at the magnificent, well-manicured lawn. It was only the third week of March, but the grass was already dark green and healthy. Tiny shrubs, colorful plants and flowers strategically framed the circular driveway. A spectacular view of the Potomac River was visible just to the left of his house.

Once she stopped the car and put it into Park, she sprinted out of the vehicle and ran to the front door. She rang the doorbell, alternating with knocking furiously. Just when she thought she was going to have to call for help, she spied a blurred figure approaching through the purposefully distorted frosted glass door and it finally swung open.

Her breath caught in her throat at the sight of a bare-chested Cam. His feet were also bare, and he wore black jeans that hung low on his lean hips. In one hand he held a black shirt carelessly. His frown quickly turned into a smile.

"Angela, what are you doing here? I didn't expect to see you until tomorrow night."

"You called me." Her voice came out in a rush as relief flooded through her at the sight of him. "Why?"

"Oh." He scratched his chin as if thinking. "I just wanted to ask if you liked Thai food."

"Thai food?" She stared at him in disbelief. She had nearly had a coronary because he wanted to know if she liked Thai food!

"You could have just called me back."

She frowned at his logical retort. "I *tried* to call you, but you didn't answer your phone."

"Oh." He glanced down at his smooth, bare chest, drawing her attention there, as well. "I was probably in the sauna. I never take my phone in there." He stepped aside. "Come on in."

"Thanks." She walked inside and he closed the door behind them, motioning for her to follow him down the black-and-white-tiled hallway into the living room. She noticed his back was just as defined as his muscled chest, and to stop from touching him, she linked her fingers together in front of her. Lord, she wished he'd put on his shirt to remove the temptation to caress his smooth, hard muscles.

"Were you worried about me?" he tossed over his shoulder.

"No," she quickly answered before sitting down on the sofa.

"No?" He treated her to a skeptical stare before sitting closely beside her. "Then why are you here?"

Why did he have to sit so close? Why hadn't she chosen one of the tan wing chairs across from the sofa? Gosh, he smelled good—clean, spicy and woodsy. She clasped her fingers tighter together as they lay in her lap to keep them from tracing the well-defined muscles of his pecs that were silently, yet loudly, inviting her to explore to her heart's content. She bit her lower lip to keep in the groan of appreciation that wanted so desperately to escape from her mouth as her eyes drank in their fill of his magnificent physique.

"Angela?"

"What?" She gazed into his eyes, certain he knew where her deviant thoughts had taken her. It just wasn't right for one man to be so sexy or so handsome.

"Were you worried about me?" he asked again with a knowing smile.

"I was concerned," she slowly admitted. "I had visions of you passed out on the floor."

"And you took time out from your busy day to check on me." He covered her hands with one of his, and a bolt of awareness shot through her. "I'm flattered."

She shrugged dismissively. "It's no big deal."

"It is to me." His voice slid over her, caressing like fine silk. "This was quite a drive from Washington."

"I made good time." She tried to remove her hands from his, but his fingers tightened, refusing to release their grip.

"But still—"

"Feel free to put your shirt on." Darn, why had she said that? Now he'd know how much his fit physique was disturbing her—and, Lord, was it disturbing her! To add insult to injury, he had the nerve to grin, revealing those stunning dimples of his. Oh boy, she couldn't take much more of this man's innate charm or outward beauty.

"You're a nurse. Don't tell me a bare chest is embarrassing you." A patient's bare chest? No. But Cam's smooth, muscled, dark brown skin? Definitely.

"Of course not. I just thought you might be—" she paused "—cold."

He laughed outright before a sensual grin turned up the sides of his mouth. "Believe me, the last thing I am sitting next to you is cold."

"I…um…" He shifted closer, and she managed to free her hands and placed one to her suddenly constricted throat. *Oh, please don't let him touch me again, or I'll combust on the spot.*

"In fact, now that you're here, feel free to examine me thoroughly."

Without answering, she quickly stood and placed some much-needed distance between them. Walking over to stand by one of the bay windows, she took in deep gulps of air to steady her rapidly beating pulse.

"Are you okay?" She heard the humor in his voice that matched his amused eyes when she turned to look at him.

"Yes, I'm fine." She tried valiantly to appear cool and unmoved by his sensual teasing, but knew she failed miserably.

"You'll get no disagreement from me on that point." His eyes slowly moved over her, setting off little violent eruptions of need in their wake.

Before she disregarded common sense and flung herself into his arms, she tore her gaze away from his and fingered a crystal vase sitting on a nearby table. Then she glanced around the room while mentally ordering herself to get it together. She noted the comfortable furnishings. The walls were blinding-white stucco with a high vaulted ceiling and high-polished red-oak flooring, half covered by a tan-and-white throw rug. Her eyes lingered on the white baby grand piano situated to the far right of the fireplace before returning to connect with the depths of Cam's eyes.

"Your house is gorgeous." It was a deliberate way to change the subject.

"Thanks." Leaving his shirt carelessly draped over the back of the sofa, he stood and walked over to her, every nerve ending in her body at attention as he approached. She felt like prey being stalked by a hungry lion. "It's home."

"I pictured you living in a bachelor pad." She tried to keep the conversation light and impersonal.

"That's not me." He stopped a few feet away from her. "I like comfort, room to roam around in and privacy. This place gives me that and is still close enough to the office and Washington proper."

"All this space for just one man?" She cocked her head at him. "Doesn't it get lonely?"

"No, I enjoy my own company." He paused before taking another step closer and adding, "Perhaps one day I'll find someone special to share it with, though."

"I'm sure a lack of female companionship isn't one of your problems." That slipped out before she could stop it.

"What does that mean?"

She sighed. "Just that any woman would feel lucky to spend time with you." He smiled as though pleased with her answer, and she admitted, "You're quite a catch."

His expression changed, and she wondered why. "Because I'm rich?"

"No, because you're a nice man and you have a great personality." The smile reappeared at her words. "You're fun to be around."

"Is that right?" His eyes slowly investigated every feature of her face, traveling down her body and detonating little explosions of awareness within her before finally returning to stare into her now-dilated pupils.

"Yes." She wished he'd stop staring at her as if she were his favorite food that he couldn't wait to devour.

"Thank you." He walked closer until only inches separated them. Suddenly she felt the need for some fresh air before she did something embarrassing like swoon at his feet. "But *any* woman just won't do," he continued softly. "I'm afraid I'm very choosy about whom I spend my time with."

"Are you?" It took every ounce of self-control she possessed not to touch him. They were so close she could feel the heat radiating off his bare skin, caressing hers, silently inviting her to touch, explore and taste. She took a step backward, and her back encountered the window, informing her she was out of space to maneuver.

"Yes, I like to surround myself with *real* people who know what they want and aren't afraid to go after it." He stepped forward, erasing the rift she had purposefully created between them. "That's why I'm looking forward to spending more time with you."

"You think I know what I want out of life?"

"Don't you?" She definitely knew what she wanted professionally, but personally—that was a different story altogether. When she remained silent, he unexpectedly offered, "Would you like a tour?"

She blinked and then said, "That would be great, but I need to get back to the hospital."

"I understand." He leaned away from her, and she instantly missed his warmth. "You have a standing invitation."

"Thanks." She maneuvered carefully around him to retrieve her purse from the sofa.

"Can I tempt you with something?" He smiled mischievously. "I was just about to fix some lunch."

"No, thanks. I've got to get back for a staff meeting."

"Okay." He slowly walked toward her, eating up her oxygen with each step he took. "Thanks for checking on me."

"Sure."

"I'm sorry I worried you."

"I'm glad you're okay and that you're following doctor's orders and resting." She breathed a little easier as she slipped back into her professional mode.

"I told you I would. Didn't you believe me?"

"Let's just say that I'm pleasantly surprised you are being a good boy."

"Normally I'm not, but I have motivation to be." He ran a hand lightly down her arm before grasping her hand. "Very lovely incentive."

"I need to leave now."

"If you must." He reluctantly released her hand. "See you tomorrow night."

If she had any sense, she'd cancel their date. Her strong reaction to his immense charm was disquieting, but she knew if she tried to back out now, he would unleash more of his abundant charm against her until she gave in again, and frankly, she didn't think her heart could take that; therefore, she would go on *one* date with him as she'd promised, but that was it.

"Bye, Cam." She turned and walked out into the hallway. He followed her to the front door where she glanced at him and softly ordered, "Next time, answer your phone."

"I'll keep it by my side." He made an X over his heart with a finger—a spot her lips longed to taste. "I promise."

Without another word, she left. Once she reached her

car, she glanced at the door and found Cam watching her with a hungry grin that curled her toes. Managing a small smile, she got into her car and drove away before she succumbed to an insane urge to throw herself in his arms and kiss that constantly smiling mouth of his. Oh, heaven help her!

The next night, Angela studied her reflection in the mirror and nodded in satisfaction. Cam hadn't told her where they were going, and she had no idea how to dress. She had chosen a simple short-sleeved knee-length black dress with a sweetheart neckline. You could never go wrong with a little black dress. She ran fingers through her short hair until she was satisfied, and then put on a silver charm bracelet on her left wrist and silver hoop earrings.

Her stomach was churning nervously, and she placed a hand there, silently chiding herself to calm down. For goodness' sake, she was just going to dinner with a casual friend. A casual friend who made her insides feel as wobbly as Jell-O.

The doorbell chimed, and she turned from the mirror and quickly walked into the hallway, not stopping until she reached the front door. Her hand on the doorknob, she took several calming breaths, smoothed her hair and opened the door.

Her breath hitched at the sight of Cam. He was dressed casually in black pants, a dark gray shirt and gray blazer. As usual, his charming expression produced his to-die-for dimples.

"Hi, gorgeous."

"Hi." She stepped aside. "Come in."

"Thanks."

"Thank you," she responded when he handed her a

bouquet of lilacs. She brought the flowers to her nose, deeply inhaling their light fragrance. "They're lovely."

"Not as lovely as you." Appreciative eyes ran over her, infusing heat throughout her wobbly body.

"I didn't know where we were going. I hope I'm dressed all right."

"Perfect," he assured her.

"Let me put these in water." She backed away toward the kitchen and motioned to the living room. "Make yourself at home."

When she looked up from getting a vase out of the cabinet and arranging her flowers, he was leaning against the door frame, watching her with an expression that turned her knees to jelly.

"Where are we going?"

"It's a surprise." He held out a hand, and after a second's hesitation, she walked over and took it.

"Okay."

"Ready?" At her nod, he led her back to the front door and followed her out. "Then let's go."

A short while later, they were seated in a crowded karaoke bar. Cam ordered hot wings, blue cheese dressing and cheese fries for them. Glancing around the picturesque bar, she laughed and took a sip of her iced tea. His choice of eateries was completely unexpected to her.

"What's so funny?"

"Nothing." She shook her head. At his continued stare she elaborated, "When you asked me to dinner, I imagined something different."

"Like?"

"A fancy five-star restaurant," she admitted.

"Disappointed?"

"No, not at all," she said quickly. "This place is great."

"Are you sure?" He watched her closely. "We don't have to stay—"

"Cam, it's fine," she assured him, and sighed contentedly. "In fact, it's perfect. I'm already unwinding from my grueling day."

"Me, too," he agreed.

"What do you mean, you too?" She pointed an accusing finger at him. "You were *supposed* to be resting today, not exerting yourself."

"I was resting. Honest." He held up three fingers of his right hand in a Boy Scout pledge. "But I was anxiously anticipating our date tonight." He winked at her. "And that was very taxing."

"Oh, I see."

"Were you?"

"Was I what?" She took a bite of a fry and chewed while awaiting his response.

He leaned closer and asked, "Were you anticipating our date?"

"I was so busy I really didn't have the chance to think about it." That was a *teeny* exaggeration, and she sensed he knew it. She'd spent the majority of the day obsessing about what to wear tonight.

"Right." He made quick work of his own fry and grabbed another one.

"I didn't."

"I believe you." She had the feeling he didn't in the least. They were silent while he chewed on a wing, and she ate more fries before he wiped his hands on a napkin and stood. "I'm going to sing. Don't go away."

Angela's eyes widened, and she gasped. "You're going to sing?"

"Yes, ma'am." He walked away and bolted onto the stage.

She watched with her mouth open, thinking he must be joking. However, he chose a song and waited for the music to start. When it did, he began singing Bon Jovi's "Livin' on a Prayer."

Angela sat forward expectantly to watch what she thought would be a typical mediocre performance. Boy, was she wrong. He had a very good voice. He sang as if he'd been born with a microphone in his hand, and his dancing wasn't bad, either. He immediately got into the song, and so did the boisterous crowd. Angela grew hot just watching him gyrating his hips, dancing across the tiny stage and really putting everything he had into his performance as if his life depended on it.

She quickly began clapping her hands and dancing in her chair as she watched his performance. Soon she noticed women were swooning over him—some going as far as to stand in front of the stage shamelessly reaching for him, clapping and cheering him on as if they were at a rock concert and he was the main attraction. She couldn't blame them. He was a handsome devil, having left his jacket on the back of his chair before going onstage. His long-sleeved shirt clung to his hard muscles, leaving little to the imagination about his fabulous physique.

She felt a twinge of something that seemed like jealousy, which quickly turned to pride when she remembered he was her date, not theirs. He slowly ran his hand over his gorgeous bald head and stared straight at her and winked, knocking her heart out of its normal rhythm. Lord, the man oozed sex appeal, and when used in full force, it was deadly. She willed her breathing to regulate as she watched the remainder of his act.

All too soon, as far as the crowd was concerned, he finished and they lauded him with huge applause, whistles, cheers and pats on the back as he made his way back to the table where he picked up his beer and downed half the contents in one swig.

"Whew! That was hard work."

"You were great!"

"Thanks." He took a smaller drink. "In another life, I wanted to be a singer."

"Really?" At his nod she asked, "Did you ever pursue it?"

"Nah, I thought it best to concentrate on a more stable career." He admitted, "My friends and mother readily concurred."

"Any regrets?"

"No, I love corporate law."

"That's how I feel about nursing. It's great having a career that you enjoy, isn't it?"

"There's nothing better. I can't imagine getting up every day and hating going to work."

"Me, either."

"You're enjoying your new position being in charge, then?"

"Very much," she answered. "It's tons of work, but I'm thriving on the daily challenges."

"I hear you're doing a great job." He grinned at her startled expression.

"From whom?"

"I have my sources," he said mysteriously, biting into a wing.

"Alesha?" She nodded knowingly.

"I'm not saying." He made a zipping motion across his mouth, causing her lips to curve into a half smile.

"I'll bet you're happy Derrick's campaign is behind you so you can concentrate on your law firm."

"It was a lot of fun and even more work, and I did neglect my practice, which is why I've spent quite a bit of time getting back on top of things. I'm happy to report the ship is again sailing in smooth waters now."

"That's good."

"It's great, because now I can concentrate on getting to know you better without any interruptions vying for my time."

"You make it sound like a priority."

"It is—rather, you are," he readily agreed. "You're my number-one priority."

She liked the sound of that. She told herself that she shouldn't, but she couldn't help it, she did. She couldn't remember the last time anyone had considered her a priority. It was nice to feel wanted, even though she had no intention of allowing anything more than friendship to develop between them.

"I'm flattered," she finally responded.

"We're going to have fun together, Angela," he said, treating her to one of his infectious dimple-laden grins, which turned positively mischievous. "Starting tonight."

Her lips twitched in humor at the glint in his eyes. He was definitely up to something. "What are you thinking, Cam?"

He leaned forward. "Who says I'm thinking anything?"

"I do. I can see the wheels spinning in your head."

"Okay." He held up his hands in surrender. "You got me."

"Well?" She waited for him to go on.

"What I'm thinking is…" He paused, grinned from ear to ear, and pointed to the stage. "It's your turn."

"Oh, no." Her smile quickly deflated, terror lighting up her eyes. "I don't think so."

"Aw, come on, you can't come to a karaoke bar and

not perform. Besides, you said you liked the place, so prove it."

"Cam…" She placed a hand to her suddenly thudding heart and nervously glanced around the packed room. "I'm not going up there in front of all these strangers." She vigorously shook her head. "No way."

"Why not?" He refused to give in. "There's no pressure. Everyone is here to have fun."

"I know, but—"

"No buts for you, remember?" He touched her hand. "Let loose tonight, Angela—for me."

His sexy plea melted her insides, and she found herself weakening. Why was it so important to her not to disappoint him? This man really upset her equilibrium.

"I don't have a very good voice."

"This isn't a talent competition," he chided. "This is just for pure unadulterated fun. When was the last time you let loose and just had fun?" Longer than she cared to admit, she realized.

"I don't know what to sing," she hedged.

"I'll choose a song for you."

"Cam, I really *can't* sing." She tried again to beg off, but he wasn't having any of it.

"Neither can half the people here." He then offered, "I'll sing with you."

"That's sweet of you, but I don't—"

He squeezed her hand, and she could tell he wasn't going to take no for an answer. "Come on."

She had no choice but to follow as he easily pulled her from her seat and led her to the stage. She stood there trying not to visibly tremble while he chose a song for them. Once back at her side, he took her hand and squeezed her fingers reassuringly.

She whispered in his ear, "What are we singing?"

"You'll see." He nodded at the teleprompter, where the title of the song appeared: "I Knew You Were Waiting (For Me)" by Aretha Franklin and George Michael. "Remember, this is just for fun, so stop looking so terrified," he whispered as the music and words started scrolling across the screen.

Despite his reassurance, at first she was nervous, barely opening her mouth, but soon got into the festive mood because Cam wouldn't settle for anything else. They flirted with each other as they danced and sang, and Angela soon forgot the crowd. It felt as if she and Cam were the only two people in the room despite the cheering for them.

She was off-key occasionally, but no one seemed to mind because she and Cam were really into the song and were flirting outrageously with each other. To her surprise, the song ended much too quickly, and they received more cheers and applause when they were done.

Cam hugged her close and whispered in her ear, "You were great."

"Thanks to my excellent partner, I was passable."

"Aw shucks, thanks, ma'am." They laughed giddily as they left the stage.

His arm remained around her waist while they walked back to their table. He held out her chair, and she gratefully sank into it.

"That was so much fun," she said.

Cam wore a satisfied expression. "I told you it would be."

"You were right." She took a big drink of tea. "I can't believe I did that."

"I can, and you were outstanding."

"I don't know about that." She laughed at his high praise. "We were good together."

"I have the feeling singing isn't the only thing we're going to be good at together." Her breath caught at the roguish glint in his eyes. "I can't wait to share other experiences with you, babe—more private performances, so to speak."

"Cam, stop it." She was suddenly hot all over, and not due to the physical exertion she had just undergone, but rather, to the burning heat of Cam's gaze directed solely at her.

"Stop what?" He reached across the table and covered her hand with his. "I'm just stating the truth."

She shook her head at him. "Has anyone ever told you you're incorrigible?"

"My mom," he said with another one of his signature grins. "But I thought women liked bad boys." His thumb rubbed back and forth across the sensitive flesh of her inner wrist, sending delicious shivers of awareness through her.

"Some do, but most of us prefer dependability."

"Baby, I'll be whatever you need me to be." He stared deeply into her wary eyes and said, "On that you *can* depend." Searing heat infused Angela's body at his easily uttered words and suggestive expression.

If she hadn't known it before, she knew now that this man, with his unending supply of charm, was going to be very hard for her to resist. It was going to be harder still for her to remember exactly why she wouldn't allow herself to become entangled in a romantic relationship with him.

Staring into his playful eyes sparkling with mischief, she knew she had inadvertently bitten off more than she could chew when she had agreed to go out with him. Oh boy, she was in deep trouble, and its name was Cameron Stewart.

Chapter 4

When Cam and Angela arrived back at her house after their date, he insisted on walking her to the door, which she secretly loved. He was a true gentleman—opening doors for her and holding out chairs all night. Chivalry, it seemed, wasn't dead. That was another mark in his favor, not that he needed one. He just couldn't be as perfect as he seemed.

"I'd invite you in, but I have to be up early tomorrow," she said, once she unlocked the door.

"I understand." He seemed reluctant to let the evening end, and she understood the feeling. "Did you have a good time?"

"I had a great time," she replied truthfully.

"You're not just saying that, are you?"

"No, I mean it. Tonight was the most fun I've had in a long time." She leaned against the door. "How about you? Did you have fun?"

"Of course I did." He touched her cheek softly. "I was with you." Her heart fluttered. Darn, this man was so effortlessly appealing!

"Thank you for a lovely evening, Cam."

"Thank you." He took her hand in his and stared deeply into her eyes, nearly hypnotizing her. "I'd like to see you again."

"I…" She couldn't bring herself to answer any way except truthfully. "I'd like that." His handsome face lit up.

"Tomorrow night?"

"I can't. I'm working a double shift."

"Saturday?"

"Okay."

"I'll call you about the time."

"Fine."

They stared at each other silently. The attraction between them was as thick as molasses. She wondered if he was going to kiss her, and he did—briefly on the cheek, much to her disappointment.

"Good night." He ran a solitary finger down her cheek where his lips had fleetingly caressed, causing a shiver of longing within her.

"Good night, Cam."

She went inside, leaned against the door and sighed happily. She had to admit this date had definitely been worth the wait. She had no intentions of entering a serious relationship with anyone, but if she did… She deliberately didn't finish that thought and pushed herself away from the door forcefully.

"Just friends, Angela. You don't have the time or fortitude for anything else," she sternly reminded herself again. *"Just friends."*

The next day, Angela met Alesha in the hospital cafeteria for lunch. Alesha looked radiant, and Angela was happy for her friend.

"Not that I need to ask, but how are married life and motherhood treating you?"

"Wonderfully," Alesha cooed. "I've never been happier."

"It shows, and I'm happy for you."

"Thanks. Your turn will come."

"I'm already happy," Angela said, and that was the truth, although part of her would like to find what Alesha had found—too bad she didn't think that would ever happen for her. And she was fine with that, she firmly reminded herself. "I wish you had brought D.J. with you."

Alesha laughed at her obvious disappointment. "I'm not good enough for you, huh?"

"Of course you are," Angela said quickly. "It's just that I haven't seen my godson in a couple of weeks, and I miss him."

"He was sleeping when I left," Alesha said. "Why don't you come to the house for dinner tonight?"

"I wish I could, but I can't. I have to work."

"What about tomorrow night, then?"

"That's not good for me, either. I have a date."

"You have a date?" Alesha choked on her water, eyes widening in shock.

"Don't sound so surprised," Angela admonished, laughing and patting her friend on the back.

"It's just that you haven't been on a date in ages. Who's the lucky man?"

Angela hesitated before answering. "Cam."

"Cam Stewart?" At Angela's reluctant nod, Alesha smiled brightly. "Well, it's about time!"

"That's what he said when he very persistently asked me out." A smile turned up the corners of Angela's mouth at the memory. "Saturday will actually be our second date."

"Second?" Alesha wagged a finger at her. "You've been holding out on me, girlfriend."

Angela laughed. "I have not."

"Then why am I just now learning about you and Cam being an item?"

"We're not an *item*," Angela denied. "We're friends, nothing serious."

"Mmm-hmm." Alesha treated her to a stern look. "You know I'm not buying that, don't you?"

Angela shrugged. "It's the truth."

"Cam's a good man."

"I know he is, but we're just friends."

"That's a good place to start." Alesha refused to be dissuaded from her matchmaking endeavors, and Angela smiled but remained silent. "Oh, Angie, you want to spend the rest of your life alone?"

"What's wrong with being alone?" Angela asked defensively. "Just because I'm alone doesn't mean I'm lonely or that I'm unhappy."

"That's not an answer to my question," Alesha said gently.

"I'm not in the market for a serious relationship," Angela insisted.

"Maybe you aren't, but—"

"I'm beginning to dread that word," Angela interrupted with a loud sigh.

"What word?" Alesha frowned, and Angela waved a hand dismissively.

"Oh, nothing. Go on with your thought."

"I know you've had a few disappointing relationships, but just remember, nothing ventured, nothing gained."

Alesha, as her best friend, knew a little about her past mistakes where men were concerned; however, no one really knew the entire sordid mess that had been her family life before moving to Washington for a fresh start.

"Cam and I have been on *one* date."

"And you're already going on your second," Alesha reminded her.

"Neither of us is looking for, nor do we want, a serious relationship," Angela stressed. "We're *friends,* and that's all we'll ever be."

"Just keep an open mind." Alesha patted her hand. "That's all I'm saying."

Angela sighed but made no further response because Alesha wouldn't believe her anyway. She'd enjoy spending time with Cam, but she wouldn't get serious, because nothing good would come from that. It never did.

When Cam arrived at her house in Georgetown to pick up Angela Saturday night, he was dressed in a navy designer suit. He held a bouquet of what Angela guessed must have been no less than two dozen red roses, which he handed to her.

"Thank you." She took the flowers, touching the soft, velvety petals before asking, "I guess no karaoke tonight?"

"I thought we'd go a little more uptown. Are you game?"

"I am."

"Good." He eyed her red flowered maxi dress with side slits approvingly. "You look beautiful."

"Thanks." She motioned to the flowers in her hand. "Let me put these in water."

"Take your time. Our reservation is for eight o'clock, so we have some time to kill."

"Okay." She pointed to the left with her free hand. "Why don't you wait in the living room? I'll be right in."

"Will do." He followed her directions and disappeared from sight.

When she returned from the kitchen, Cam was slowly walking around, taking in the ambience of her home. She wondered if he noticed the lack of family photographs. Instinctively, she knew there wasn't much that would escape his legally trained mind. He turned and smiled when he found her watching him, but remained silent. She placed the large vase of flowers on the end table.

"Can I get you a drink?" she offered, to dispel the uncomfortable silence.

"No, I'll wait until we reach the restaurant." He glanced around briefly again. "I like your house."

"Thanks, it's home."

"That's all that matters."

"It is." She took as much of his intense stare as she could before lowering her gaze.

"How long have you lived here?"

"Eight years." She pretended interest in arranging her roses in their vase. "The neighbors are nice, and it suits my needs. More importantly, it's close to the hospital."

"Please, don't mention that place," he groaned, and turning to face him again, she laughed.

"Sorry…speaking of my place of employment, how have you been feeling?"

"Never better," he said. "I went back to work for a few hours yesterday."

She placed a hand on her hip. "Cam, didn't Dr. Jackson tell you to take a week off?"

"He did." He held up a silencing hand. "But I can't sit around doing nothing. It's not in my DNA."

"Men!" She shook her head at him.

"Don't give me that. I'm sure you're the same way," he accused with a grin.

They stared at each other, and a smile broke out across her face, followed by tinkling laughter. He had her pegged just right.

"I can't deny it." She chuckled. "I am."

"I thought so," he replied triumphantly.

"Just promise me you won't overdo it."

"I won't." Before she knew it, he was standing in front of her, touching her face lightly. "I like that you worry about me."

"I…" Her voice failed her. He was much too close for her to think of an appropriate response. "Shouldn't we be going?"

Cam studied her so intensely that she felt like an insect under a microscope. He must be an excellent lawyer because with just a look, he seemed to stare straight through to her soul, uncovering all of her carefully hidden secrets. It was very unnerving.

"I guess we should," he finally answered, taking her hand and bringing it to his lips before leading her out.

Their destination ended up being Giovanni's, a lovely Italian restaurant. The place was packed, and they sat in a secluded booth off to one side of the room. The lighting was dim and romantic. The wooden tables were covered with white linen tablecloths, upon which lay strategically placed silverware, and their red wine was served in crystal goblets. It was a far cry from the loud, boisterous atmosphere of their first date.

A waiter immediately appeared and took their order before disappearing again. He returned a short while later with their drinks before leaving them alone again.

"So, what do you think?" Cam watched her investigate their surroundings.

"It's charming."

"I'm glad you like it."

"Who wouldn't?" She paused as their food was placed before them. Boy, that was fast. "I love Italian food."

"I know."

Her forkful of spaghetti halted in midair. "How do you know?"

"Oh, I have my ways." He laughed. "Remember?"

"Alesha?" She lowered her fork to her plate.

"Maybe." At her perplexed look, he asked, "What's wrong?"

"Nothing." She wasn't sure if she was comfortable with her best friend discussing her with him.

"We were just engaged in friendly conversation at dinner last night, during which you happened to be one topic." He read her thoughts. "We weren't gossiping about you, Angela."

She smiled and chided herself for making a molehill into a mountain. "I believe you."

"That's good." He nodded, satisfied. "I wish you had been there. We had a great time." He paused and chuckled. "That is, until D.J. took it upon himself to spit up on me."

"He didn't!" Angela grinned in amusement.

"He did," he said wryly.

"Oh, I hate that I missed that." She giggled. "I'll bet your expression was priceless." She finally brought her forkful of spaghetti to her mouth and moaned in appreciation. After swallowing, she asked, "Aren't you going to try your food?"

"I am." Cam picked up his own fork. "I was just enjoying the beautiful view."

"I haven't been here before." She twirled more spaghetti around her fork. "It's nice, isn't it?"

Piercing eyes met and held hers. "I wasn't talking about the restaurant."

"Oh." She nervously smoothed her bangs to one side. "Thank you."

"You're welcome." She suddenly felt that familiar heat begin to engulf her body that manifested whenever she was in his presence. "You have no idea how gorgeous you are, do you?"

"How am I supposed to answer that?"

"You're not." His breathtaking dimples made an appearance. "It was a rhetorical question."

"I'll bet you're a force to behold in the courtroom."

He shrugged. "I do all right."

"I'm sure you do." Her fingers toyed with the stem of her wineglass, but she didn't drink the wine. "Why did you choose corporate law instead of criminal?"

"I thought about criminal long and hard—both sides. If I became a defense attorney, I'd run the risk of defending someone who was guilty, and I hate being lied to."

"Doesn't everyone?" Cam's eyes narrowed at her bitter tone, but he didn't make any mention of it, thankfully.

"If I went the prosecutorial route, I'd run the risk of inadvertently sending someone innocent to prison, and I couldn't live with that."

"That would be terrible," Angela agreed.

"So I decided on corporate, and I love it. The constant finagling really appeals to me."

"How long have you been in private practice?"

"Eight years. It took more hard work than I care to remember, but I finally built my baby into one of the biggest firms in the state," he said proudly.

"Now you can enjoy the fruits of your labor."

"Yeah." He stared deeply into her eyes. "All I need is someone to share them with." What did he expect her to say to that?

She took the easy way out and changed to a safer subject. "I'll definitely have to come back here. I love the ambience, and the food is fabulous."

"I thought we'd move up from the karaoke bar." Cam finally cut into his lasagna, and she heaved a sigh of relief that he wasn't going to press her to respond to his previous statement.

"I had a marvelous time there, but I have to admit, I'm enjoying the cuisine here much better." She chewed a mouthful of spaghetti and swallowed before stating, "I make a mean spaghetti and meatballs, but this takes the cake." She paused and then said, "I'll bet you're thinking that all I do is eat."

"Not at all," he replied after swallowing a bite of lasagna. "It's a pleasure to be with a woman who doesn't pick at her food because she's afraid of gaining an ounce."

"I work out a lot." She laughed and added, "I really have to because of my lifelong love affair with food."

"Well, your routine definitely works because you have the perfect figure."

"Oh, I wouldn't go that far."

"I would." Appreciative eyes raked up and down from her head to her waist. "You have a body that curves and I'm sure caresses in all the right places." She coughed loudly at his erotic assertion, and he laughed. "Are you okay?"

"Fine." She took a much-needed sip of her water and then tried to steer the conversation to safer territory. "How's your food?"

"Great." He didn't seem the least bit interested in dinner, but rather was intent upon eating her up with his ravenous eyes.

"Mind if I taste your lasagna?"

"Nope, help yourself." He laughed because she was already spearing a forkful and bringing it to her mouth. "How is it?"

"Oh, God, that's wonderful!"

"Have some more," he offered, and his laugh intensified because she was already in the midst of procuring another bite.

"Don't mind if I do." She rolled her eyes heavenward. "I'll definitely have to come back here."

"We'll make a point of it." He implied she would be coming with him, and she rather liked that implication.

"Here, try some of mine." She twirled some spaghetti and offered it to him. He took it, his eyes never leaving hers, chewed slowly and then swallowed. Her hand remained suspended for several seconds before she swallowed hard and lowered her fork to her plate. Lord, it was sexy feeding him.

"Mmm." His eyes darted to her slightly parted lips before returning to stare into hers. "Delicious."

She shivered from desire and fought an urge to push their plates aside, climb across the table and fasten her hungry mouth to his tempting one. What was the matter with her?

"What are you thinking, Angela?" She had a feeling he knew *exactly* what forbidden thoughts were racing through her mind.

"Nothing." She choked out the single word.

He leaned forward and whispered, "You can tell me."

She'd like to tell him. No, scratch that. She'd like to *show* him. Oh nuts! This man was absolutely too handsome, too likable and too dangerous to her resolve to remain emotionally unattached.

"I was just thinking that I like you." His smile informed her he knew that hadn't been all she had been thinking. "You're a nice man."

"I'm glad you feel that way because that means you'll be amenable to more dates with me." He reached across and covered her hand with his and confessed, "I like you, too, very much."

Glancing into his mesmerizing eyes, suddenly food

was the furthest thing from her mind. After a long, intense silence, she blinked and withdrew her hand from his.

"As a Southerner, I learned an early appreciation for food." She tried to dispel the sexual tension between them.

"You're from South Carolina, right?"

"Right."

"Any family there?"

"Some." When she didn't elaborate, she was aware of him studying her guarded expression.

"I'm from Atlanta, where my mom's family still lives." She could have kissed him for not pressuring her to talk about her dysfunctional family. He really was an intuitive, thoughtful man. "I have a huge family."

"Did you call your mom about your accident?" She seized the opportunity to steer clear of her troubled childhood.

"Not yet."

"Cam…" she scolded.

"I've been trying to get my strength back so that I can withstand the lecture she's going to give me about the dangers of fast cars and for not calling her the second the accident happened." He sighed at the thought. "I'm going to call her in a day or so." At her raised eyebrow, he placed a hand over his heart. "I promise."

"At least when you do call, you can honestly tell her you're okay."

"The best news I'm going to tell her is that I've met a wonderful woman." His statement both warmed her heart and sent shivers of apprehension down her spine.

"You don't know enough about me to come to that conclusion."

"That's not true," he quickly contradicted. "I know I

feel completely at ease when I'm with you, and you make me happy. That's more than enough."

"I feel the same way," she admitted.

"That's perfect." His response was designed to put her at ease. It didn't.

"Is it?"

"Absolutely," he said. She was surprised at his next statement, a change of subject. "I would think as a nurse, you'd be lecturing me on bringing you to a restaurant loaded with saturated fat and tons of carbohydrates," he teased.

"I'll forgive you." She laughed. "Don't get me wrong, I believe in eating right, but I have to indulge myself from time to time."

"Is that right?" His expression turned absolutely decadent. "I'll have to make sure I'm around during your indulgent times. I'd love to indulge in sin with you any time you're ready." He smiled at her wickedly, informing her he knew exactly the havoc he was wreaking on her equilibrium.

She shook her head at him and chuckled softly. "You are a mess, Cameron."

"I could be your mess." He leaned forward and covered her hand with his. "Would you like that?" Her breath caught in her throat as she stared into his serious eyes.

"I…I'm not sure," she slowly answered.

"No pressure." He released her hand and took a drink of his wine before asking, "What are you going to have for dessert?" She blinked. He had a knack for keeping her off balance.

"You're trying to make me gain five pounds tonight, aren't you?"

"I just want you to have whatever you want tonight." He stared at her beguilingly. "What do you want tonight,

Angela?" She wasn't going to touch that question with a ten-foot pole.

"I think I'll try the tiramisu." His slow, knowing smile warmed her insides until she felt ready to ignite.

"Tiramisu it is."

She exhaled jerkily but remained silent. What she had expected to be a casual date had suddenly changed into something more. What was it about this man that made her uncharacteristically needy?

Staring into Cam's mesmerizing eyes, she knew she was very close to doing the one thing she had promised herself not to do—fall for him, and after just two dates. Oh darn!

Chapter 5

When Cam and Angela left the restaurant, neither was ready for the night to end, and they decided to go dancing. They drove a short distance to Eighteenth Street and pulled up outside of a very exclusive club. Cam walked around the car and took her hand after handing his keys to the valet. Being a Saturday night, it was insanely crowded.

"This place is impossible to get into, Cam." Angela eyed the long line of people waiting to be admitted. "Are you sure you don't want to go somewhere else?"

"We'll get in," he stated confidently, strolling past the throng of people.

The doorman smiled as they approached. "Hi, Mr. Stewart."

"Hi, Dan." Cam patted the man on the back. "It's busy tonight."

"The more the merrier."

"Absolutely," Cam agreed, ushering a completely impressed Angela in without any hesitation.

The hostess immediately walked up to them when they entered. "Mr. Stewart, your usual table?"

"Yes, thanks, Mary." Cam placed a hand on Angela's back as they followed Mary across the crowded room and up the stairs to a remarkably secluded balcony overlooking the dance floor.

"You must come here a lot to have your own table."

"Some." He shrugged noncommittally.

"What can I get you to drink?" Mary asked.

Cam glanced at Angela. "May I order for you?"

"Of course."

"Champagne, Mary. The best."

"Yes, sir." Mary nodded obligingly and left.

"Champagne," Angela echoed. "You're going to spoil me."

Cam winked. "That's the plan."

In no time, their champagne was delivered. The waiter poured them each a glass before replacing the bottle in its bucket and leaving.

"To long-overdue beginnings." Cam touched his glass to Angela's. She'd barely taken a sip and placed her full glass on the table when Cam reached for her hand and suggested, "Let's dance."

"Let's." She took his proffered hand and stood.

Cam stopped once they were in the middle of the massive throng of people occupying the dance floor. They started to dance amid the laughing, jumping crowd, and Angela felt free and uninhibited. Unfortunately, after a couple of fast songs, the band decided to change the tempo to slow, seductive and romantic. Without hesitation, Cam pulled her into his arms until her soft contour was plastered against his unbending length.

"Relax." Cam smiled down at her. "I promise I won't bite—not unless you want me to." He chuckled at her quickly indrawn breath, and he leaned closer and seductively asked, "Do you want me to?" She wisely didn't answer that question.

"Did you plan this?" she asked instead.

"What?"

"The sudden change in music selection."

"How would I have anything to do with what music the band plays?" She wasn't buying his innocent facade for a second.

"I don't know, but you seem to be well-known here and carry a lot of sway." Tilting her head thoughtfully, she asked, "Why is that?"

"Okay." He grinned and admitted, "You've got me. I'm part owner."

Her eyes widened in shock. "Are you kidding?"

"No. I bought into the club a couple of years ago."

"No wonder we've been getting such preferential treatment."

"Is that a bad thing?" he teased.

"No, it's…" She shook her head in awe. "You're just full of surprises."

"Oh, babe, you have no idea, but one day you will," he promised mysteriously.

"What does that mean?"

"You'll see." He pulled her closer and ordered, "Now be quiet and just feel me."

Dear Lord, how could she *not* feel him when he had her pressed tightly against his rock-hard body? She had to admit, they fit perfectly together. Cam's hands rested possessively on her lower back, keeping her exactly where he wanted her. When his thumb slid back and forth along her spine, Angela groaned inwardly and gave in to the impulse to twine both arms around his neck, allowing them to move impossibly closer as her heart pounded fiercely against her chest.

"Are you feeling me yet, Angela?" At his soft yet potent question, her head rose from his shoulder and she stared into his confident eyes.

"Yes." She sighed, and he smiled as if pleased with her truthful answer.

"Good." He lightly brushed his lips against hers, making her long for more.

Unable to withstand the blatant desire evident in his hungry stare, she laid her head back on his shoulder and did as he ordered—just felt.

When they arrived back at her house in the wee hours of the morning, he walked her to her front door, but neither made a move to go inside. The beautiful starry sky was the perfect backdrop to what had been a perfect date.

"Thank you for a wonderful evening."

Cam outlined her bottom lip with a finger. "It doesn't have to be over with yet."

"Cam…"

"What?"

"I have to be at work early tomorrow."

"That still leaves us hours to…" he paused before suggestively ending "…spend together."

"I don't think so, Cam."

"Why not? You want to."

She couldn't deny his confident assertion, so she didn't try to. "What I want isn't always good for me."

"I promise I'm the exception to that rule."

He might well be. However, did she want to risk finding out? She had lousy taste in men, but could her luck be changing with Cam? He wasn't like anyone she had ever met; however, if she let him get too close and things blew up as usual, she had the feeling he would hurt her more than anyone ever had, and that was what she was trying so hard to avoid.

"Angela." He stared into her wary eyes. "Why are you so afraid?"

"Because I've had terrible luck in the relationship department," she confessed after a long silence, and received a tender look in return for her honesty. "Horrible luck."

"*Had* is the operative word," he stressed. "I'm not like anyone you've ever dated before, Angela."

Amusement lit her eyes at his statement. "Very arrogant, aren't you?"

"I prefer the term *confident*." He smiled and ran a soothing hand down her arm. "You were simply dating the wrong men for you. In fact, I'll venture to say they weren't men at all, but rather boys."

"I can't argue with you there."

"Tell me about them." She stared into his kind eyes and realized she wanted to tell him. This wasn't a conversation she'd intended on having on her doorstep, but he had asked.

"I'll spare you the gory details and make it short and sweet, even though the reality was anything but. One was a boyfriend in college. I came into some money and he professed his undying love for me, proposed and we got engaged. He was more than halfway through my inheritance before I realized he was just using me. I shut down the gravy train and kicked him to the curb." She spoke in a clinically detached voice, but they both knew the incident had scarred her. "The second was an intern at the hospital—who, I found out just in the nick of time before he ruined my career, was a junkie more interested in using my access to the medication cabinet to frame me for his thefts than in me." She smiled cynically, squared her shoulders and promised in a hard voice, "I don't intend to ever be used again."

"That's good, because I have no intention of doing that." His thumb caressed her jaw. "Ever. Do you believe me?"

"I don't know." She closed her eyes briefly before

opening them again and firmly replying, "What I do know is that I'm not rushing into anything."

"All right." His hands fell away from her, and she instantly missed his comforting touch. "Fair enough."

"All right?" She blinked rapidly. "You're giving up?"

"Don't you want me to?" he countered.

"Yes." The one word was drawn out slowly.

"Then you should be satisfied."

She wasn't in the least, and had a feeling he knew it. "I am."

He chuckled at her somewhat dazed expression. "Don't worry, I'm only agreeing to go home." He ran his hands down her arms and back up, sending shivers of delight through her. "I don't intend to rush you, Angela. You can have all the time you need."

"Time to do what?"

"Admit to yourself where we're heading."

"Where's that?"

"You'll see." He kissed her good-night briefly on the lips, too briefly, before releasing her to unlock her door. "Sleep tight."

"Good night," she whispered before going inside alone.

April 9, the two-week anniversary of her first date with Cam, and Angela's birthday, dawned with sunshine, and Angela knew it was going to be a wonderful day. However, that assertion soon diminished when no one remembered her birthday—not a single soul.

A little after one o'clock, while sitting in her office staring out at the annoying sunshine and picture-perfect blue skies, her phone rang. Her irritated eyes gravitated toward the annoying instrument before she reluctantly picked it up.

"Hello?"

"Happy birthday, Angela!"

"Alesha." Angela's sad face quickly transformed. "I thought you had forgotten."

"Of course I didn't forget," Alesha chided. "I'm sorry I didn't call you earlier, but D.J. has had me running around like a crazy woman this morning," she groaned, and Angela laughed.

"I don't believe it. That little angel is no trouble at all."

"Ha!" Alesha scoffed. "He's my baby and I love him, but he's too much like his father."

"I'm going to tell Derrick you said that," Angela threatened.

"I'll deny it," Alesha quipped, and they both laughed. "I wanted to take you to lunch, but the day has gotten away from me."

"No problem. It's been a madhouse here today, so I just grabbed a bite from the cafeteria."

"Oh, how I remember those days." Alesha laughed.

"Don't you miss them?"

"Sometimes," Alesha admitted. "But I wouldn't change my life now for anything."

"You're so domesticated, it's sickening," Angela replied playfully.

"Don't I know it." Alesha chuckled. "Listen, I was going to ask you to dinner, but Derrick just called and we have to have dinner with another senator and his wife."

"Oh." Angela's face fell, and she was glad Alesha couldn't see her. "Don't worry about it. I understand."

"I know it will be a day late, but how about we celebrate tomorrow?"

"It's a date."

"Do you have plans for tonight?" Alesha asked hopefully, "Maybe with Cam?"

"Not with Cam, but I do have plans." She told another white lie. She didn't want Alesha worrying about her. "As soon as I get out of here, I'm partying with friends."

"That's good," Alesha said. "I'll call you tomorrow and we'll work something out, okay?"

"Okay." She heard D.J. begin crying in the background. "Go and take care of my godson."

"My little darling is so demanding." Alesha sighed before ringing off.

Angela replaced the phone in its cradle and sighed heavily. Well, at least Alesha had called. She had been looking forward to celebrating with Alesha the way they always did for each other's birthdays, and now she knew that wasn't going to happen, at least not tonight. Oh well, she was a big girl and it wasn't the end of the world. She could use a quiet night at home anyway.

When the phone rang again, she picked up the receiver and answered listlessly. "Hello?"

"Hi, doll, what's wrong?"

"Cam?" She immediately perked up on hearing his voice. "Nothing's wrong. It's just been a hectic day. How are you?"

"Great now that I'm talking to you." A bright smile lit up her face.

"You flatterer."

"Just stating the truth, darling." She could hear the smile in his voice and wished she could see those adorable dimples of his. "I know this is short notice, but I was hoping I could see you tonight."

"I thought you had a business meeting?"

"I did, but thank God it was canceled so now I can spend the evening with you." His words were music to her ears. "So are we on?"

"Yes," she accepted. She had fun with him, and fun was definitely what she needed tonight.

"Excellent. I'll pick you up at seven, how's that?"

"Perfect. How should I dress?"

"Casual." He paused and added, "Jeans."

"Karaoke again?"

"I'm not telling, but I think you'll enjoy what I have planned."

"I'm sure of that."

"Count on it," he promised. "I'll see you tonight."

"I can't wait."

"Mmm, I like the sound of that." Her toes curled at his sexy voice. "Bye, doll."

"Bye." She hung up, and for the first time that day, a bright smile lit up her face. She couldn't wait until tonight.

Promptly at seven o'clock, Angela's doorbell rang. She opened it to reveal a smiling Cam. He brought her the customary beautiful bouquet of flowers—this time white tulips.

"I'm going to have a flower garden on the inside if you don't stop bringing me flowers," Angela quipped as she let him inside.

"No can do." He kissed her cheek, and she flirted with the idea of turning her head and capturing his mouth, but she didn't.

After placing her flowers in water, they exited the house. They were dressed similarly in jeans and white shirts, but Cam wore a jean jacket.

As they walked hand in hand to his car, Angela glanced at her unruly lawn. "I really have to do something about my lawn."

Cam followed her gaze. "It's not that bad."

"It will be if I don't get a handle on it. My yardman moved away, and I haven't had the time to replace him. If I don't do something soon, the neighbors are going to kick me out."

"I think you're safe." He laughed. "It just needs a little trimming."

"Yard work is not my thing," she admitted. "I'd better start looking for someone seriously before summer really hits."

He opened her door to his black Jaguar convertible and helped her inside before walking around and getting behind the wheel. Once he started the car and reversed out of the driveway, he glanced her way.

"Prepare yourself for major fun tonight," he promised.

"Oh, I'm more than ready," she informed him, and he grinned in approval.

"That's what I like to hear."

"Is this your permanent new car?"

"Yeah." He shrugged. "I guess."

"You don't sound very enthused." She eyed the luxurious black leather interior. "What's wrong? This is a gorgeous car."

"I know."

"But?" she prompted.

"But I miss Yvette," he said sadly.

"Why didn't you get another Corvette, then?"

"It just wouldn't be the same." He shook his head. "No other car can replace Yvette. She was one of a kind, custom-made." He added wistfully, "We'd been through a lot together."

"I'm so sorry." She patted his arm comfortingly. "Just try to think of the good times you two had." She tried to keep the humor out of her voice but knew she had failed when he briefly glanced her way.

"You're laughing at me, aren't you?"

"No. Really, I'm not."

"I see that smile," he accused, and unable to contain it a second longer, she burst into laughter.

"I'm so sorry." She wiped a tear from the corner of her eye. "I didn't mean to laugh."

"It's all right." He chuckled along with her.

"I really don't mean to be insensitive." She dabbed at her eyes.

"There's not an insensitive bone in your body." Cam brought her hand to his lips and then changed subjects. "By the way, on the way here, I realized I left my wallet at home. Do you mind if we stop at my place to pick it up?"

"I can pay," she offered, and laughed when he grimaced as if she had wounded him.

"No way."

"I don't mind paying, Cam." She turned in her seat slightly to smile at him playfully. "Don't tell me you're one of those men who balks at allowing a woman to pay."

"Of course I'm not," he denied, glancing at her. "You can pay when you invite me out."

"Why not now?"

"Because I invited you, so I'm paying. I'm sure it's a written rule that whoever invites pays."

"It is not." She shook her head at him. "What kind of logic is that anyway?"

"Man logic," he replied proudly. "And you're not going to get me to go against it."

"Okay." She lifted her eyes heavenward and gave up trying to dissuade him. "You men and your *man logic*."

"Like you ladies don't have yours."

"Touché."

They reached his place shortly, and she was surprised when he walked around and opened her door. She hadn't expected to get out. At her questioning gaze, he replied, "I had a waterfall installed in the backyard I want you to see."

"I'd love to." She took his hand and stepped out. "Your yard is so gorgeous."

"Yours will be, too, once it gets a little attention," he said.

"I don't think it will ever compare to yours, but I'd settle for nicely mowed grass and trimmed hedges," she joked.

"Well, that's not too much to ask for." He leaned close and whispered, "Maybe the yard fairy heard you."

She crossed her fingers. "I sincerely hope so."

They walked into the dark house still holding hands. He led her through the dimly illuminated halls toward the back of the house, where he flipped a light switch once they reached the backyard. What seemed like thousands of green firefly lights illuminated the darkness, reflecting off the pool, dancing off the trees, the grass, shrubbery and a large white tent set up on the far end of the lawn.

"How pretty." She gazed around at the dancing artificial lights. "What's in there?" She pointed to the tent.

"I'll show you." He led her toward the temporary edifice.

When they walked inside, it was dark, but not for long. As if on cue, bright lights illuminated the interior. Angela gasped as her eyes encountered the bright, colorful birthday decorations. Before she could say a word, people jumped out, including her coworkers and Alesha and Derrick. Angela fell back against Cam's chest in shock, a hand going to her heart.

"Surprise!" everyone yelled in unison.

"Oh my—" Angela's words were interrupted as she was swarmed by her friends.

"It took all my resolve not to spill the beans when I called you today," Alesha said. "But I didn't want to ruin your surprise."

"I was bummed out because I wouldn't be celebrating my birthday with you," Angela admitted.

"I'm sorry." Alesha hugged her tight. "Forgive me."

"There's nothing to forgive." Angela glanced around at the gaily decorated tent and then turned to Cam. "You knew it was my birthday?"

"Of course I did." He grinned, and intense emotion squeezed at her heart. "We've had this party planned for a week."

"A week?" She glanced from Cam to Derrick to Alesha. "You guys are the best. I can't believe you went to all of this trouble."

"Cam took care of everything," Alesha happily told her best friend. "He wouldn't let us pay for a thing."

"You shouldn't have." She turned her full attention to Cam as Alesha and Derrick discreetly walked off and shooed everyone else away from Cam and Angela.

"I wanted to."

"But Cam…" She glanced around at the lavish surroundings—ice sculptures, champagne fountains, huge cake and tables of catered food to feed an army. "This is too much. You shouldn't have spent so much money on me."

"Why not?" He playfully tugged a strand of her hair. "I can afford it."

"That's not the point. I don't want you to—"

"Angela, you need to learn to accept a gift. Okay?"

She hesitated before reluctantly agreeing. "Okay. Thank you."

He treated her to a dazzling smile. "You're welcome."

"Hey, birthday girl." Alexis, a friend from work, along

with several other coworkers, flanked her. Alexis smiled at Cam. "You don't mind if we steal her away for a bit, do you?"

Angela sensed that Cam did mind, but he smiled back and replied, "Not at all."

"We won't keep her long," Alexis promised as they led Angela away. "So Angie," Alexis cooed once they were out of earshot. "Who is that hunk throwing this lavish party for you?"

"Just a friend."

"I wish I had a *friend* like that—" Alexis glanced around at Cam's house appreciatively. "Filthy rich and movie-star handsome."

Angela's eyes narrowed. "It's not about how much money a person has, Alexis."

"Of course it isn't."

Angela bit her tongue to keep silent the retort that sprang to her lips.

"So how does it feel to be thirty-one?" Alesha wisely changed the subject.

"Good. Last year was the traumatic one." Angela made a face and then laughed. "This year's sublime compared to that, and thank goodness I haven't noticed any crow's feet yet."

"Girl, you're not getting older, just better," Alesha proclaimed.

"Amen!" The group of women chorused together, raised their glasses in a salute.

"Now, back to that man." Alexis's one-track mind kicked in. "If you're not serious about him, can you direct him my way?"

"Alexis…" Angela's eyes narrowed perceptibly.

"Girls, excuse us for a few minutes." Alesha pulled

Angela away before she could finish what was sure to be a scathing sentence.

"Thanks for the save." Angela gave Alesha a wink.

"No problem." Alesha chuckled. "I thought I'd better get you out of there before you went postal on Alexis."

"You know I like her, but she just goes crazy when a handsome, wealthy man is in sight."

"And you don't want her poaching on your territory, right?"

"Cam and I are just friends, Alesha."

"There are friends, and there are *friends*."

"Alesha." Angela shook her head. "You are such a matchmaker now that you're happily married."

"Guilty." Alesha laughed. "I can't help it though. You and Cam are so cute together."

"Alesha, we're just—"

"Dating," Alesha finished for her with a grin, which turned to a chuckle at Angela's exasperated sigh.

"Keeping each other company," Angela corrected.

"Protest all you want, but all I know is that the temperature in the room rises when you two look at each other," Alesha said. "You could have something special with Cam—if you allow yourself to."

"Maybe." Angela chewed her lower lip and then admitted, "I don't know if I want a serious relationship. I like the way my life is right now—my career is firing on all cylinders, and frankly, I'm not sure if I want to rock the boat by overextending myself."

"Just keep an open mind," Alesha urged. "You've had some disappointments, but Cam's different from the jerks that broke your heart." Angela silently agreed with her. She had a feeling he was more dangerous to her heart than all the other men she had known combined—if she let him be, that is. "I think you've already come to that conclusion. Haven't you?"

Angela remained silent as her eyes sought out Cam's across the room. He smiled at her, and she smiled back. Her heart fluttered and butterflies tap-danced in her stomach. Oh boy. Cam was the kindest man she had ever met, and she *did* enjoy his company—a lot. For self-preservation's sake, she was trying to keep things casual between them, but darned if he wasn't making it nearly impossible for her to do that.

Chapter 6

Cam stood alone, gazing at Angela across the room. She smiled at him, and his heart somersaulted in his chest. Man, he really had it bad for her. Out of the corner of his eye, he saw Derrick approaching.

"Did your date abandon you?" Derrick asked.

"No." Cam's frown deepened. "Some friends spirited her away."

"Don't look so forlorn." He slapped Cam on the shoulder. "They'll bring her back."

"If they don't, I'm going to go and get her," Cam promised darkly.

"You seem serious about her."

"Why does that surprise you?"

"Because you took your sweet time in asking her out." Derrick took a swig of his drink. "I thought you had decided she wasn't your type."

"Oh, she's my type all right," Cam quickly responded. "Besides, I'll have you know it's your fault I haven't dated her seriously before now."

"Me?" Derrick brought a hand to his chest. "How is it my fault?"

"Because I was busy getting you elected to the senate," Cam pointedly reminded him. "All my energies, time and talent were directed toward you, my friend."

"And I appreciate your loyalty and dedication." Derrick grinned. "She must be pretty special for you to not lose interest in all that time."

"She is special." Cam's gaze returned to Angela, who appeared to be talking seriously to Alesha. "I like her a lot."

"Why?"

"Why?" Cam refocused on his friend with a wry grin.

"Yes, it's a simple question. What do you like about Angela?"

"Well, Mom, let me see...." Cam's sarcastic rejoinder elicited laughter from Derrick.

"Speaking of Mama Mabel, did you call her yet?"

"Yes, and a phone call wasn't good enough." Cam groaned at the memory. "It took an hour-long video chat to convince her that I wasn't lying in a hospital bed near death, and that I'm in my right state of mind."

"Well, the latter is debatable," Derrick quipped. "Is she heading this way?"

"I don't think so." Cam scratched his chin. "Her social schedule is very busy right now." He chuckled at the memory of his mother relating all the church activities she was engaged in presently. "She gets around more than I do."

"She is vibrant for a sixty-six-year-old, and if I know her, she'll be visiting soon to check on you for herself," Derrick predicted.

"I know you're right," Cam agreed. "I'd love to see her, but I don't want to be mothered—especially not when I'm busy cultivating a new relationship."

"Speaking of that, you never did tell me what's so special about Angela," Derrick reminded him.

"Well, for one thing, she's genuine. She doesn't play at being anything that she's not. I'm so tired of being around women who are fake from the top of their heads down to the tips of their toenails. Angela's not like that—what you see is what you get."

"And obviously what you want."

"I do," Cam quietly agreed. "She's like a fresh breath of air, Derrick. I love being around her. When I'm with her everything just feels—" he searched for the correct word "—right."

"I've never heard you talk like this about any woman."

"Exactly!" Cam nodded vigorously when Derrick's words proved the point he was trying to make. "I've never felt like this before. When I'm with her, something in me just clicks into place."

"What else do you like about her?"

"That's not enough?" Cam continued without hesitation. "She's not looking for a man to take care of her. She has her own career, which is very important to her. She's driven and is as much of a workaholic as I am."

Derrick cocked an eyebrow. "That's hard to believe."

"I know, but she is." Admiration glinted in his eyes. "She's also fun to be around. She enjoys simple pleasures and doesn't care how much money I have. In fact, I think my wealth unnerves her."

"And that's a good thing?"

"Yeah, after the women I've dated who were only interested in the size of my bank account, it's a very good thing."

"Well, your bank account is huge."

"I know, but Angela couldn't care less about that. When she asks about my work it's because she's interested, not because she's trying to gauge how much money I make, and thus, how much I can afford to spend on her. I know not all women are gold diggers, but I'm so tired of women coming on to me simply because I'm a lawyer with my own firm and a nice house," he lamented. "Do you know that for our first date, I took her to a karaoke bar?"

Derrick's eyebrows rose. "And she went out with you for a second date?"

"Yes, she did." Cam grinned at his disbelieving friend. "I'll have you know we had a great time and even sang together."

"Oh no!" Derrick placed a hand to his head in mock horror. "She didn't feed your professional singer fantasy, did she?"

"For your information, she thinks I have a great voice." Cam paused before happily summing up, "We're good together."

"Well, counselor, it sounds like you're completely hooked."

"I'm not a fish," Cam replied drily.

"No, but you're hooked just the same." Derrick patted his shoulder and then laughed. "Looks like I'll have to dust off my penguin suit soon."

"Whoa, not so fast, we're taking this nice and slow."

Derrick gasped in disbelief. "I know you, and that's definitely not your style."

"Angela's gun-shy, and I don't want to scare her off, so I'm giving her time to realize what a catch I am." Cam winked immodestly.

Derrick chuckled. "How considerate of you."

Cam shrugged. "I'm a considerate guy."

"And a little bit delusional," Derrick couldn't resist adding.

"Go dance with your wife," Cam ordered. "And while you're at it, send my date back."

"Will do." Derrick smiled and sauntered away.

Cam glanced in the direction Angela had been, but

she wasn't there anymore. As he scanned the room for her, someone touched his arm, and he turned to find his date by his side again.

"Hey, birthday girl." He took her hand in his. "I just sent Derrick to tear you away from Alesha. Are you having fun?"

"Yes." She treated him to a smile that would light up the world. "I can't believe you did all this for me."

"I'd do it again to see you smile like that."

"You're such a nice man, Cam."

"Shh," he whispered. "I don't want to ruin my reputation."

"Your secret's safe with me." She kissed his cheek and whispered in his ear, "Thank you."

"Making you happy is all the thanks I need." He kissed her hand. "Come on, let's party."

"I'm so ready." Her fingers tightened in his as they walked over to the makeshift dance floor on the patio to join the fun.

"What were you and Alesha talking about?" he asked, pulling her into his arms.

"You and me," Angela slowly admitted. "What about you and Derrick?"

"The same."

"I know they mean well, but this is the main reason I've shied away from dating people my friends know."

He nodded in approval. "So you admit we're dating?"

"Casually," she clarified.

"I agree with that."

Angela's eyebrow rose in surprise. "You do?"

"Mmm-hmm, but I'm warning you."

"What?" she asked warily.

"I'm looking for more than a casual fling with you, Angela."

She tensed up at his easy assertion, and he pulled her closer instead of allowing her to escape. "Cam…"

"That doesn't require a response from you, so don't say anything." He grinned infectiously. "Just concentrate on having fun."

"That, I can do." She relaxed a little in his arms.

He winked at her. "And it's my job to see that you do."

"Then carry on," she softly ordered.

"Yes, ma'am." He swung her around, twirled her away and pulled her back close.

The remainder of the party was filled with gifts, food, cake, dancing and pure fun. Alesha and Derrick were the first to leave, and the party went on for a couple of hours after, with the rest of the group reluctantly departing until only Angela and Cam were left.

Angela silently admitted it was the best birthday she had ever spent, and it was all because of the wonderful man standing beside her.

"Let me help you clean up." Angela began gathering plates, which Cam took from her and returned to the cluttered table.

"No way." He took her hand and led her into the house through the patio, not stopping until they were sitting side by side on the sofa. "I have a cleanup crew coming by in the morning."

"I had the best time tonight."

"That was the plan." He reached inside his jacket pocket and pulled out a rectangular white box with a silver bow. "Happy birthday."

"Cam. You've already done too much. You didn't have to buy me a present."

"I know I didn't *have* to. I wanted to." He placed the box in her hand. "Open it."

"But Cam..."

"I can't take it back."

She arched an eyebrow at his assertion. "Can't or won't?" She slowly unwrapped the box, revealing a gold charm bracelet from which different types of flowers dangled.

"Both." He watched her lift the bracelet from its blue velvet interior. "Do you like it?"

"It's so beautiful, but it's way too much. I—"

"What did I tell you earlier about learning to accept a gift?" He took the bracelet from her fingers and placed it on her wrist. "There, that's perfect."

"I don't know how to thank you." She lightly fingered the lifelike, intricate charms.

"That's okay. I do."

"How?"

He didn't speak, instead framed her face with his hands and captured her mouth with his. This kiss wasn't fleeting contact like before. It wasn't teasing or exploratory, but rather a thorough, spine-tingling kiss designed to melt any and all opposition.

Resistance wasn't an option—in fact, it never occurred to her. She had wanted to experience Cam's kiss for days, and now that she was, she wasn't disappointed. His mouth demanded, her lips parted and their tongues met halfway in a thorough examination, which both eagerly participated in.

Her hands gravitated around his neck as she moved and she was pulled closer to his hard body. She turned sideways and felt like crawling onto his lap to disintegrate any unacceptable distance between them. Lord, when had a kiss ever made her feel or want so much? His pleasure-evoking hands roamed down her back as their lips slanted one way and then another, trying to taste every luscious centimeter of each other's mouths. Tongues and lips played and chased as the kiss went on and on.

He groaned as she capitulated, and then just as quickly dueled with his tongue—or was it her groaning? She didn't know. She couldn't tell which feelings were hers and which were his. They felt like one being, wanting the same thing, feeling the same thing and needing the same thing to survive—more of each other.

When they eventually parted, both were breathing hard. Her eyes were tightly closed as she fought for some semblance of control, which seemed intent upon eluding her. His next huskily spoken words didn't help her waning restraint, either.

"Stay with me tonight, Angela," he whispered against her well-kissed mouth.

At his not unpleasant suggestion, her eyes flew open. God, she wanted to say yes. She wanted that more than anything, which is why she knew she couldn't. Things had quickly gotten out of hand. They had only dated a few times, yet she felt bereft when they weren't together, and when they were, she was happier than she had ever been. She was so afraid if she gave in, the world would implode, and she was intent to avoid that at all costs. She needed to slow things down.

"I can't."

"You want to." His eyes seemed to stare through to her soul, and she was unable to look away. "I know you do."

"It's too soon, Cam." She stared into his eyes, which was a mistake because the blatant desire contained therein nearly made her combust.

"I know it is," he finally agreed on a sigh. "But—"

"Uh-oh, here comes that but," Angela groaned, and he chuckled.

"But I want you." He pulled her closer and nipped at her thoroughly kissed lips. "And you want me."

"Cam—" His mouth effectively silenced her feeble protest. They enjoyed a long, spine-tingling kiss that left her knees weak and sent her heart thudding rapidly against her rib cage.

"Angela, stay."

"I—I can't." From somewhere, she mustered the strength to refuse him and the gnawing hunger his kisses had unleashed within her. "I can't."

"Okay." He reluctantly released her and stood. She stared up at him, flabbergasted.

"You're giving in?"

"Disappointed?" Hopeful humor lit up his eyes as she stood to face him.

"Surprised," she substituted.

"I can wait for you, Angela, because you're worth it."

"Oh." Darn, this man had a magnificent knack for effortlessly saying and doing the right things.

"Come on." He took her hand. "I'll take you home before I change my mind." At the front door he turned and asked, "You haven't changed yours, have you?"

"No." Her soft response was forced from her mouth, which curved into a half smile at his disappointed expression. "I haven't."

"Okay." He sighed in resignation. "Home it is."

When they arrived back at her house, the neighborhood was quiet, save the nighttime insects going about their business. Always the gentleman, he walked her to the front door and carried her birthday loot inside for her, placing the presents on the hallway table.

"Would you like to stay for a nightcap?"

"I don't think that's a good idea, unless you're asking me to stay the night."

She smiled at his hopeful expression and shook her head. "I'm not." *But Lord, I want to.*

"Then I'll take a rain check."

"Okay, I understand."

"Was it a happy birthday, babe?"

Her insides melted at his endearment. "Yes, thanks to you."

"Good." His arms encircled her waist. "I'll call you tomorrow." He glanced at the wall clock behind her. "Well, later today."

"Okay." Her fingers played with the lapels of his jacket. She didn't want him to go but was afraid to let him stay.

"Good night."

"Good night, Cam. Thanks again for my party and my present."

"It was my pleasure." He winked. "Well, almost."

She laughed. "You are so bad."

"One day soon, you're going to find out just how bad I can be." He kissed her quick and hard before walking away.

Angela followed him outside, waving when he glanced at her through the lowered car window before driving away. Sighing, she went inside and closed the door. She knew she had made the wisest decision in sending Cam away, but that didn't stop her from wishing she had made a different one.

The next day was Sunday, and Angela had the entire day off, which was a rarity for her. She celebrated by sleeping late. She awoke with a smile, stretched like a lazy cat and opened her eyes to face a sunshiny day.

Sliding off the bed and padding barefoot toward the kitchen, she made a beeline for the coffeemaker, plopping a K-Cup in.

Stifling a yawn with the back of her hand, foot tapping impatiently on the white linoleum, she waited for her coffee to brew, which thankfully didn't take too long. Grabbing her black mug, she inhaled deeply before taking a grateful sip of her French roast coffee.

Plodding over to the sink, she stared out the kitchen window at the gorgeous day. Her smile fell, and her mouth dropped open in shock. She blinked rapidly several times, but the image was still there. Cam was outside mowing her lawn!

Without considering her skimpy attire, and with her coffee mug still in hand, she sprinted out the back door across the slightly damp grass. Cam was dressed in a white T-shirt and blue jean shorts that stopped just below his knees. He had on a black baseball cap and tennis shoes. She had never seen him more casual or cuter.

Walking up behind him, she tapped him on the shoulder. "Cam, what are you doing here?"

He turned around. Appreciative eyes slowly traveled over her, making her aware that she was dressed in her pj's, which consisted of a pink spaghetti-strap tank top and matching shorts. He smiled the lazy, gorgeous smile she was growing to love before shutting off the mower.

"What did you say?"

"What are you doing here?" Angela repeated her question, when what she really wanted was to run into the house and put some clothes on.

He glanced at her nearly completely mowed lawn. "Isn't that obvious?"

"You shouldn't be mowing my lawn."

"I wanted to do it." He took the cup from her unresisting fingers and sipped her coffee before returning it to her. "While I don't mind your current state of almost undress, you might want to change before you give the neighbors an eyeful," he suggested around a chuckle when she defensively crossed her arms over her chest.

"I was surprised to see you here," she explained, glancing down self-consciously. She wondered why she didn't burst into flames from the fire of his gaze. "I'll be right back."

"You don't have to. I'm almost finished."

"Okay." She backed away and motioned to the lawn with one hand. "Thank you for doing this."

"You're welcome."

"Come in before you leave?"

"I will."

She ran inside and heard the mower start up again. She didn't stop until she reached her bathroom, where she stripped, showered and changed into red shorts and a black T-shirt in record time. Twenty minutes later, he knocked on her kitchen door and she let him in.

"The lawn looks great." She glanced around him at the neatly trimmed grass. "Thank you."

"No problem." He sat down at her tiny kitchen table and stretched out his long legs in front of him.

"Cold drink?"

"I'd love some water." He watched as she took out a glass and filled it with ice water before returning to sit across the table from him. "Thanks." He took the glass and downed the contents in one long gulp.

"More?" Her hand gravitated toward his empty glass.

"No, thanks. I'm good." He intercepted her hand and entwined her fingers with his, sending goose bumps up her bare arm.

"I can't believe you mowed my lawn." She attempted

a laugh, but it came out airy. "My neighbors will be as delighted as I am."

"I didn't do it for your neighbors." He stared deeply into her eyes, and she felt raw. "You know that. Don't you?"

Lord, he could undo her with just a simple look or an innocent touch. "What are your plans today?"

His teasing smile let her know he was aware she was trying to change subjects. "I don't have any." His fingers continued playing with hers. "Why?"

"I was…" She took a deep breath for courage and then continued, "I was wondering if you'd like to spend it with me."

"Are you asking me out?"

"I guess I am." Her heart thudded while she waited for his response.

He smiled. "How can I refuse?"

"Good. Go home and change and then come back."

He released her hand and glanced at himself. "I need a shower, huh?"

She laughed. "I didn't say that."

"No, but I do." He chuckled, standing. "I'll be back in a couple of hours."

"I'll be waiting." She stood and walked him to the door.

"You won't have to wait long," he promised, and squeezed her fingers before leaving.

She watched him load the white twin-cab pickup with the lawn mower and other yard tools. He climbed into the cab and waved at her before driving away.

Angela leaned against the door with what she knew was a sappy expression on her face because Cam, by taking time out of his day to do something nice for her, had demonstrated—without fanfare and without expecting something in return—that she mattered to him. He effortlessly made her feel special, and that was a feeling she could definitely get used to, if she allowed herself to.

Cam was masterfully chipping away at the carefully constructed walls protecting her trampled heart, and as of yet, she hadn't found an effective means to counter his sensual, protracted assault. More importantly, did she really want to? Sighing heavily, she ran fingers through her hair as she thoughtfully chewed on her lower lip.

Did she want to keep fighting her attraction to Cam? That was the sixty-four-thousand-dollar question. Wasn't it?

Chapter 7

Two-and-a-half hours later, they walked up to the movie box office to buy tickets for the recent sci-fi flick they both had been wanting to see.

Angela frowned when Cam took out his wallet. "What are you doing?"

"Paying for the tickets."

"Nope, I invited you." She handed her credit card to the attendant before he could, and received their tickets. At his distasteful expression she reminded him, "These are your rules. You said when I took you out, I could pay."

"I know, but if my mother finds out I made a lady pay for our date, she'll skin me alive."

"I won't tell her," Angela promised, taking his hand and leading him inside. "Come on, let's get some snacks."

"Okay, I'll pay for those."

"Oh, no, you won't." Angela shook her head when Cam sighed heavily. "Get used to it, buster. Today you're not paying for anything."

"This isn't my idea, Mom. I promise," Cam whispered, mortified.

"Come on." Angela steered him toward the snack bar with a laugh.

After buying their snacks, they entered the theater and were delighted when both expressed their preference for sitting in the back. The theater was half-full, but they were the only ones in their row.

"I can't believe you're a sci-fi buff." Angela sipped her diet cola as the first preview flitted across the screen. "I can never find anyone to go with me to see sci-fi. All of my friends like horror or romantic comedy."

"You won't have that problem anymore." He offered her some popcorn. "Anytime you want to go, just give me a call."

"What if you're busy?" Angela plopped a few pieces of popcorn into her mouth and chewed.

"I'll never be too busy for you, Angela." She swallowed hard at his easy assertion. "Remember that."

He placed his drink in the armrest to his right and flipped up the one dividing them. Then his arm snaked around her shoulders, and he pulled her closer to his side. She didn't think of resisting because it felt too good to be so close to him. He was warm, strong and inviting, and he smelled great—like spice and bergamot. She wanted to bury her nose in his neck and overdose on his scent. Instead, she settled for laying her head on his sturdy shoulder and settling in to watch the movie.

The extra-large bucket of popcorn they shared quickly disappeared as they voraciously munched on it. Angela's fingers encountered the bottom of the bucket, scraping salt, butter and a few stray unpopped kernels. She looked for a napkin to wipe her fingers and frowned when she didn't find one.

"Did you get napkins?" she whispered to Cam.

"Uh-uh. I thought you did."

"I may have some tissues in my bag."

Cam watched her while she rummaged in her bag and triumphantly pulled out a pack of tissues. After she cleaned her fingers, he took her hand in his, and at her questioning gaze, he deliberately brought each finger to his lips, placing a tender kiss on each, ending with taking a nip out of the tip of her index finger with his strong white teeth.

Her heart fluttered at the feel of his warm breath and soft lips against her skin.

"Mmm, you taste delicious."

"Um…thanks," she whispered breathlessly.

Without saying another word, he winked at her, placed her hand on his thigh and turned back to watch the movie.

Oh, my God, how could something so innocent be so sexy? She fought with everything in her to stop from straddling his lap and capturing his mouth with hers. Somehow, she forced her eyes from him and also returned her attention to the movie, willing her heart to cease its rapid beating. After a while, her pulse rate settled down and her concentration returned, allowing her to enjoy the rest of the movie.

"That was fantastic!" Angela said as they left the theater two hours later hand in hand.

"Better than I expected," Cam agreed. "I loved the first one, but I didn't think the sequel could live up to its predecessor."

"Neither did I, but it did."

"Where to now?" he asked as they walked to his car.

"Do you like baseball?"

"Are you kidding?" He grinned. "I'll have you know, I played in high school and in college."

"Well, Washington has a game today, and I have tickets." She dug in her cross-body messenger bag and showed him. "Wanna go with me?"

"You have to ask?" He opened the car door and helped

her inside before walking around and climbing behind the wheel. "You're my idea of a dream date."

And he was hers. As usual, she was having an effortlessly wonderful time with him.

They arrived at the ballpark an hour later and took their seats, which were close to the field. Once the game started, the stadium was really crowded and noisy as fans cheered their team on. Cam and Angela soon got into the festive spirit themselves.

"Are you crazy? He was safe!" Angela yelled at the umpire before sitting back down. "That guy needs glasses."

"He's wearing glasses."

"Well, he needs to have his prescription checked," she mumbled.

"You're really into it." Cam laughed at her. "Aren't you?"

"Did you expect me not to know anything about the game?"

"Nope." At her dubious glance he admitted, "Okay. Yes. I've just never met a woman who *really* likes sports."

"How can you not like sports?" Angela sipped her water. "That's just plain un-American."

"I completely agree." Cam suddenly sprang to his feet. "Slide! Slide!"

"I'm not the only one who's into it," she teased.

"Derrick refuses to go to games with me." He grinned as he sat down. "He says I embarrass him too much."

"What's the sense of going to a game if you're not going to get involved in it?"

"Exactly," Cam agreed.

"Anytime you want to go, just call me," she offered.

"I definitely will," he said. The look he gave her stole her breath away.

"How about some peanuts?" She raised her hand to signal the peanut seller.

"Look." Cam grabbed her hand, lowering it to her lap and pointing to the giant screen on the scoreboard. "We're on kiss cam."

"So we are." Angela turned from the screen to stare at him suspiciously. "Did you arrange this?"

"How could I?" He shrugged innocently, but she still had her suspicions. When the people around them began urging them to kiss, he said, "We can't disappoint everyone." His hand curved around her neck, pulling her close, his thumb beneath her chin tilting her head up. "Can we?" Without giving her time to answer, his mouth captured hers.

She expected a quick peck but, boy, was she wrong. Cam's lips played with hers before fusing tight as his tongue invaded her mouth, engaging in a heated game of hide-and-seek with her tongue. Her nails dug into his sturdy shoulders, trying to anchor herself to the world as she reveled in the heated thoroughness of his kiss. He kissed her long and hard, and everyone around them started whistling and teasing them the longer the devastating kisses continued, but none of that forced Cam to end their embrace which, if possible, grew more intense.

When he reluctantly released her mouth, the crowd and the game were forgotten—everything except their consuming hunger for each other, which was threatening to obliterate anything and everything standing in the way of them feeding it. She realized that despite her best efforts, she was very close to forgetting her reasons for keeping Cam at arm's length, because when she was with him, her past hurts, unwavering commitment to her career—everything suddenly paled in comparison to the overwhelming need Cam unleashed within her.

She liked her life the way it was, didn't she? She didn't want to become dependent upon anyone, and she didn't want anyone depending on her—except her patients and her staff. Yet here she sat on another date with Cam, having a great time, wanting him with every fiber of her being.

Cam grinned at her as if he could read every thought and emotion racing through her, and she got the distinct impression he couldn't be more pleased with her obviously weakening resolve where he was concerned. She tore her eyes away from his and tried to focus on the game while she wondered how she had lost control so quickly, and pondered what she needed to do to get it back. The answer to both successfully eluded her.

"Thanks for inviting me to dinner, Angie." Alesha glanced around the crowded, quaint Italian restaurant. "We're long overdue for a girls' night out."

"Yes, we are, and I'm glad you could make it." Angela needed a night out with her best friend to stop herself from obsessing about her ever-growing feelings for Cam and the complications said feelings were creating in her carefully ordered life.

"Derrick was thrilled to get me out of the house so that he can spoil D.J. without me chastising him." Alesha shook her head and laughed when Angela chuckled. "He's worse than I am."

"He does love his little one."

"Yes, he does." Alesha sighed happily, and Angela grinned at the complete look of love on her friend's face. "I sound like a sap. Don't I?"

"No, you don't," Angela said, squeezing her hand. "You sound like a woman very much in love, and I'm thrilled for you."

"Thanks. I never thought I could be this happy." Alesha slyly predicted, "You'll know the feeling one day."

Angela smiled tolerantly at her matchmaking friend and said, "I'm already happy."

"You know what I mean." Alesha sipped her water. "How are things with you and Cam?"

"Good."

"Just good?"

"Yes, just good." Angela laughed at Alesha's audible sigh. "I keep telling you that we're just…" Angela's voice trailed off as her breathing stilled.

"What's wrong?" Alesha frowned.

"Um, nothing," Angela whispered, her eyes still glued to the other side of the restaurant where Cam was sitting with another woman. He had told her he had a business dinner tonight. She inwardly huffed. *Some business!*

Alesha followed Angela's gaze. "Is that Cam?"

"Yes." Angela tore her eyes away and refocused on Alesha. "That's him."

"Who is that with him?"

"His date, I guess." The words were ripped from Angela's mouth. She forced what she hoped was a dismissive shrug and coolly replied, "We're not exclusive. He's free to date whomever he wants, and so am I."

"But you don't want him dating anyone else, do you?"

"I don't care what he does." She perused the menu. Feeling Alesha's eyes on her, she assured her friend, "I'm fine, Alesha."

"We can leave." Alesha's sympathetic tone revealed she didn't buy Angela's cool assertion for a second.

"No, I'm hungry and they have wonderful food here." This was the restaurant Cam had introduced her to. It really irked her that he had brought another woman here.

Oh, God, she silently bemoaned. *I do care that he's out with another woman. I care a lot!*

"Angie, I'm sure there's a logical explanation. Why don't you go over there?"

"No." Angela shook her head. "Let's grab a waiter. I'm starving." She had been starving, but her appetite had gone right out the window upon seeing Cam with his "date."

She tried to keep her eyes away from Cam and his dinner companion; Lord knows she did, but more than once, she felt her eyes straying across the room, willing him to see her, but he didn't. He was very focused on his much younger date, who in turn was absolutely enthralled with him. They talked nonstop, laughing frequently, and his touchy-feely companion beamed at him like a love-sick puppy!

By the time she and Alesha left the restaurant, she was incensed and angry with herself for feeling that way. She had set the ground rules and insisted to Cam on numerous occasions that they were just friends, just casually dating with absolutely no strings attached to either of them. However, that truth didn't stop her from feeling betrayed.

How many times was she going to have to learn the painful lesson that serious relationships weren't for her?

Angela bristled when Cam breezed into her office the next morning unannounced, treating her to one of his gorgeous smiles that sent her pulse racing even though she was upset with him. Why did he have to be so handsome, and why did she have to be so susceptible to his devastating charms?

"Hi, gorgeous."

"What are you doing here?"

He frowned at her cold, angry tone. "I missed you,

and I wanted to see you." He walked over and sat on the corner of her desk. "What's wrong?"

"Nothing." She stood and gazed out the window, placing some distance between them and showing him her back.

"Are you okay?" He walked over to stand beside her. "You seem mad."

Give the man a cigar!

"How was your business meeting last night?" She hadn't meant to say that, but now that the question had leaped from her mouth, she turned and treated him to an accusatory glare.

"It was very good," he answered automatically, though his face held confusion.

"Great." She turned to walk away, but his hand on her upper arm halted her. "Let go!"

"What is the matter with you?" His fingers tightened on her arm when she tried to pull free. "Did I do something to upset you?"

"Why would you think that?" She glared at him. "Guilty conscience?"

"No." His frown increased. "What do I have to be guilty about?"

"What indeed?" Freeing her arm, she sat back down behind her desk. "Would you please leave?"

He crossed his arms stubbornly. "Not until you tell me what's going on with you?"

"I'm fine." She turned her attention to her laptop. "If you'll excuse me, I have a lot of work to do." He covered her hand with his, and she snatched her hand away, prompting a raised eyebrow from him.

"What is wrong with you?"

"I saw you, okay!" The words burst from her mouth like steam from a pressure cooker.

"You saw me where?"

"At dinner last night with your *date*." She stood and walked over to the coffeepot, tossing over her shoulder, "Alesha and I were at Giovanni's, and imagine my surprise when I spotted you."

"You were there?" He stood and walked over to stand beside her. "I can't believe I didn't see you."

"It's understandable. You were preoccupied," she sneered. He grinned like an idiot, which incensed her further. "Something funny?"

"Why didn't you come over to my table?"

"I didn't want to interrupt." She tried to keep her mouth shut, but her wayward tongue refused to be silenced. "You seemed so cozy."

"You're jealous," Cam announced happily.

"No, I'm not," she denied hotly.

"Well, you're doing a pretty good imitation of it."

"I just don't like being lied to."

Instead of being angry at her accusation, he seemed amused. "Angela, it *was* a business dinner."

"Sure it was," Angela snorted.

"Okay, it was part pleasure, too," Cam conceded.

An arched eyebrow rose. "No kidding?"

"The young lady you saw me with was the daughter of a friend. I've known her since she was twelve," Cam explained. "She wanted to talk to me about law school—Harvard in particular, since I went there." She studied his face carefully, glancing deeply into his eyes, and saw the truth there. "I would have invited you, but I thought you'd be bored." Her anger deflated, leaving embarrassment in its wake. "Do you believe me?"

"Yes." She offered an apologetic smile. "I'm sorry, Cam."

"Don't be. I rather like jealous Angela."

"I'm not… I wasn't…" She sighed and decided to leave that alone. Here she was, the one insisting they keep things casual, and yet she *had* been jealous upon seeing him with another woman. She needed to get herself together and fast. "I'm really sorry. Even if you were out on a date, I had no right to be jealous."

"Yes, you did—you do," Cam said with a wide grin.

"No, I don't." She sighed. "We both agreed that we're just friends."

"You agreed to that. Not me." He pulled her close, kissed her lips softly and then drawled, "I'm flattered you think I could land such a young chick."

She chuckled when he waggled his eyebrows.

"Any woman at any age would consider you a catch."

"Oh really?" Then he asked hopefully, "Present company included?"

Present company definitely included. She bit her lower lip to keep that troubling admission in her mouth.

"I apologize for overreacting. I just don't like being lied to." She tried to explain away her jealous rant and save face. "I've had enough of that in my life."

"I'll never lie to you, Angela. You can count on that." He pulled her close, gazed into her uneasy eyes and promised, "I don't cheat, either. I'm with you now—only you."

She swallowed hard at his statement. Staring into his tender brown eyes, she could see he meant that, which made her absurdly happy—and uneasy.

"Cam, we're…" She shook her head helplessly, at a loss for words.

"Don't bother denying it." His arms tightened around her waist. "You care."

She remained silent because they both knew he was right. What was worse, she had no idea how to put the train back on the track where her quickly evolving feelings for him were concerned. Lord help her, she was becoming used to having him around.

She had no intention of being burned again. That, however, seemed completely unavoidable since, like a pyromaniac, she couldn't resist the compelling flames of her scorching attraction to Cam, which seemed poised to do just that.

Chapter 8

Cam strolled into the Ritz-Carlton Hotel to attend the annual nurses' ball Angela's hospital threw for charity. To his delight, she had invited him, but he had declined because he had to be out of town on business. Upon seeing her genuine disappointment when he told her he couldn't make it, he had promised himself he would be back in time for tonight; thus, he had cut a weeklong business trip down to five days.

They had been seeing each other for a month. One wonderful month, he happily amended, during which time he had become more and more convinced that she was the one for him. He knew she cared about him—especially after her jealousy at seeing him dining with another woman. Since then, she had been more open, and he couldn't be happier about that. He purposefully never pressured her to give more than she was able to give. She liked and wanted him, and that was enough for now.

He walked farther into the elegantly decorated ballroom and immediately began searching for Angela. Eagle eyes undertook a cursory inspection of the sparkling crystal chandeliers hanging from the vaulted ceiling, the multitude of white-linen-covered tables and the shining golden-white marbled floors as they searched the beautifully dressed women until he pinpointed the object of his desire.

Angela was standing alone on the far side of the room by the buffet table, wearing a black evening gown that left her arms and a wide expanse of her upper and lower back bare. A wicked slit up one side allowed a glimpse of her gorgeous legs. She looked good enough to eat, and he was very hungry.

Wearing a wolfish grin, he determinedly made his way toward his lady—his grin widened at the thought. If she knew how hooked he was becoming on her, she'd bolt in the other direction, so he'd keep his feelings to himself for now.

The men who had hurt her before were fools, and unfortunately had warped her sense of what a real relationship should be, but he did owe them a debt of gratitude. Because of them she was thankfully unattached—a situation he planned on remedying.

He wasn't nicknamed the *pit bull* in the courtroom for nothing. He knew how to bide his time and masterfully break down obstacles brick by brick until he had achieved his goal, and that's exactly what he intended to do with Angela Brown. He'd shatter the walls she had erected around her heart so fast she wouldn't know what had hit her.

He watched as she tried to decide which hors d'oeuvre to sample, studying the tray of tasty treats as if her life depended on choosing the correct one. Walking over until he was standing directly behind her, he encircled her waist with one arm. She stiffened until he whispered in her ear, "Hey, gorgeous."

"Cam!" She turned around and flew into his arms, food forgotten. He chuckled at her enthusiasm.

"Now, that's what I call a welcome."

She pulled back a little self-consciously. "What are you doing here? I thought you were out of town."

"I was, but my trip finished up earlier than expected, so here I am. I tried to call you."

"I guess I didn't hear my phone with all this noise." She made reference to the loud music playing. "I'm glad you made it."

"Me, too." Releasing her waist, he took her hand and twirled her around, appreciatively eyeing her. "Damn, you look good."

"Thanks." She ran her hands down the arms of his black tux. "And may I say you don't look too shabby yourself."

"I hate penguin suits."

"But you wear it so well."

"I do, huh?"

"Absolutely." She straightened his tie and then gazed into his burning eyes. "Perfect."

"I could learn to like them if you keep looking at me the way you are."

"Really?" She batted her eyes innocently. "Which way is that?"

"Like you want to get me alone and—" he leaned forward and whispered the remainder of his sentence in her ear "—make a thoroughly enjoyable meal of me."

"Cam!" she gasped. "Behave."

"For now," he promised, and couldn't resist adding, "but just wait until I get you alone."

"I'm afraid that might not be possible tonight."

He frowned at her unexpected statement. "Why not?"

"I'm one of the prizes in the bachelorette auction. I wasn't supposed to be, but one of the girls chickened out at the last minute and I'm taking her place, so if I'm auctioned off, I'll have to spend the rest of the evening with my *date,*" she explained.

"You're one of the auction prizes?" Cam nearly choked on the question.

"Yep." She laughed at his distasteful expression. "What's wrong? Don't you think I'll fetch a good price?"

"You'll be the highest earner," he predicted darkly.

"Why so gloomy, then?"

"I don't like the idea of men bidding on you."

"It's for charity," she reminded him. "Besides, the prize is only one evening of my time."

"An entire evening?" he balked, and instead of dissipating, his displeasure seemed to increase. "This is getting worse by the second."

"Why, Cameron Stewart," Angela began, placing a hand on his rigid arm. "You're not jealous, are you?"

"Yes." He didn't bother to deny it.

"I'm flattered, but you don't have to be."

"I don't?" His scowl lessened, and he ran a finger down her soft cheek and watched her eyes darken with need. "Why is that?"

"Because this is strictly a business proposition and will be handled as such." That wasn't exactly the answer he was looking for, but he decided not to push.

"That still doesn't make me feel any better."

"I'm sorry. I don't know what else to say." Her eyes pleaded for understanding. "I can't back out."

He sighed and forced a halfhearted smile. "I know you can't."

"Say it like you mean it." She tried to wipe the furrow from his brow with her fingers. He captured her hand, bringing her palm to his lips.

"How can I when my lady is about to be auctioned off?" She gasped audibly at his words, and he could tell she liked being called *his*. Mmm, that was very promising. He couldn't help asking, "You are my lady? Aren't you?"

"Cam, I..." Her voice trailed off as she, along with the other nurses, was called to the stage.

"Saved by the MC." His eyes twinkled as he added, "For now." He refused to release her hand, even when she gently tugged against his fingers.

"Cam, let go."

He reluctantly complied. "Go on before I change my mind."

When she leaned in to softly kiss his cheek, he fought against hugging her tight and never letting her go, but she walked away before he could act on the impulse. She took her place on stage with the seven other women being auctioned, and a slow smile spread across his face as a brilliant idea formed in his mind.

"Now, gentlemen," the man with the microphone began. "The time you've all been waiting for, our bachelorette auction benefiting juvenile diabetes, is at hand. You'll notice each lady is holding a number, and that's how you place your secret bids. Let's *generously* remember this is for charity." He motioned to the ladies, and each stepped forward and introduced themselves before going back to their respective places in line. "Gentlemen, get your bids in, and the winners will be announced in thirty minutes."

"I feel like a piece of meat," Angela joked when she returned to Cam's side.

"Don't feel that way." He brought her hand to his lips. "Remember, you're doing this for a good cause."

"Well, you're in a better mood." She eyed him suspiciously. "Why is that?"

"Simple." He led her onto the dance floor in the center of the room. "I put in a bid for my favorite nurse."

"You bid on me?" Her eyes widened as she went willingly into his arms. "Seriously?"

"Yep."

"How much?"

His arm encircled her waist, and he pulled her tight before responding confidently, "Enough to ensure I win."

"Cam, you didn't go overboard, did you?"

"I'm not letting another man have the pleasure of your company for the evening." His hand stroked her bare back and he felt her shiver in response.

"I assure you I won't get any pleasure from it." She paused and then added, "In fact, I'm dreading it."

"You don't have to worry about it, babe, because I'm going to win." Self-assurance shone from him.

"I shudder to think how much you bid."

"Don't sweat it." He shrugged dismissively. "I can afford it."

"I know you can, but—"

"Besides, it's going to a wonderful cause."

"Yes, it is," she agreed.

"Then let's not talk about money anymore. Okay?"

"Okay." She smiled. "How was your trip?"

"Very productive." One of his hands moved low on her hip, and he smiled when she bit her lower lip to unsuccessfully suppress a groan. "I'm in the process of landing a very big new client."

"That's wonderful." The pride reflected in her eyes made him feel great. "Congratulations."

"Thanks." He twirled her away from him and then pulled her back, closer than before. "What did you do while I was gone—besides agree to be auctioned off?"

She laughed at his gentle rebuke. "Besides the usual daily grind?" She glanced around the room before refocusing on him. "I worked my fingers to the bones to get this shindig ready on time."

"You did a wonderful job, but now that I'm back, it's time for you to let your hair down and have some major fun." He waggled his eyebrows and promised, "It'll be my extreme pleasure to see that you do."

"You're so silly," she said, but her smiling expression informed him she really liked that about him.

"Life is meant to be enjoyed, babe." He nipped lightly at her lips, purposefully leaving her wanting more. "Are you with me?"

"I'm with you," she whispered.

"Then hold on for one exciting ride," he warned with a gleam in his eyes.

One dance seamlessly moved into two, and then three. They were both oblivious to everything around them as they danced and simply enjoyed being together. The need to kiss her was overwhelming, and despite the crowded room, his mouth lowered purposefully toward hers. Her arms encircled his neck, one hand resting behind his head, and her mouth met his halfway. However, before they could properly kiss, Angela was called back to the stage, along with the other nurses. Sighing, Cam kissed her quickly and softly before releasing her.

"Has it been thirty minutes already?" Angela complained.

"I guess so." Cam shrugged. It seemed as if they had only been dancing for seconds. "You'd better get up there."

"I don't want to," she confessed.

"Come on." He took her hand and walked her toward the stage. "Time to do your duty." He leaned over and whispered in her ear, "Besides, I can't wait to claim my prize."

"You really think you're going to win." She chuckled. "Don't you?"

"I know I am, baby." He winked before helping her onto the stage.

Cam took out his phone and called the chauffeur who had driven him tonight, informing him that he and his date would be leaving shortly. Then he returned his smiling attention to the most beautiful woman on the stage who, it seemed, only had eyes for him, much to his delight.

"All right, all of the bids are in and we'll start with the highest bidder by a long shot. In fact, I can safely say this one bid alone ensures that the entire evening will be a huge success." The master of ceremonies grinned and continued, "Cameron Stewart has won the pleasure of Angela Brown's company for the evening." He glanced into the audience and waved his hand invitingly. "Come on up and claim your date, Mr. Stewart."

"You don't have to tell me twice." Cam's exuberant refrain elicited loud laughter and applause as he walked up and guided a stunned Angela from the stage, whispering in her ear, "I told you I'd win."

"How much did you bid?" Angela asked again, her curiosity piqued.

"I can't tell you. It would make you too conceited." At her continued questioning gaze, he relented. "Let's just say the number started with a one and ended with a zero, and that's all I'm saying."

She shook her head at him as though he were a naughty child that she didn't quite know how to handle, and then she chuckled in resignation. "Well, Mr. Stewart, I'm completely yours for the evening. What's your pleasure?"

His arm snaked around her waist. "Let's get out of here, and I'll show you."

"I've done my duty for the night," she decided. "Let's go."

Outside, Angela expected Cam's Jaguar, but she was surprised when a black stretch limousine pulled up instead.

"Wow." Angela's eyes widened as the chauffeur opened the door for them and Cam helped her into the back of the car. "Why so formal tonight?"

"The car picked me up from the airport tonight, and I decided to keep it for our date."

"You're too much."

"I aim to please." He stretched out an arm along the back of the seat, moving closer to her side.

"You do." She moved until she was pressed up against his side, and his arm draped around her shoulders in approval.

"Show us the sights, Jim," Cam instructed the driver.

"Yes, sir."

The impenetrable privacy glass slid silently up, separating them from the world. Cam turned to Angela, his eyes feasting on her beautiful, happy face.

"I've been dying to do something all night," he confessed.

"What?" She sighed when his fingers danced along her bare shoulder.

"This." Without further hesitation, his mouth fastened on hers. She was pulled into the ferocious vortex, where they feasted as if they'd been starving for years and were suddenly privy to a succulent banquet. Angela half turned and cradled his cheek with her palm. Cam growled against her lips, sending delicious shivers through her as the kiss deepened sinfully.

"God, I needed that," he exclaimed long seconds later.

"Me, too," she whispered.

He glanced at the bottle chilling in its bucket to his left. "Champagne?"

"Yes." He released her and popped the cork, pouring them both a glass in crystal flutes, then handing one to her. "Thank you."

"To good friends." He raised his glass in a toast.

"To good friends," she echoed, touching her glass to his. She took a small sip and then sat her full glass to the side and leaned back against his shoulder. "This is nice." His arms went around her, and she snuggled even closer to him. "Very nice."

"You'll get no complaints from me." They were silent for a while until he asked, "Are you enjoying the sights?"

She giggled.

"What?"

"My eyes were closed," she confessed, turning to smile at him.

"Tired?"

"No, happy." She paused. "I really missed you, Cam."

Warning bells were blaring in the dark recesses of her purposefully sheltered heart that she was not only in quicksand but was sinking fast, but she seemed incapable of saving herself. She didn't want to care about him, but she did—a lot. It was as simple and as complicated as that.

"I missed you, too." He fingered her face and cocked a thoughtful eyebrow. "Maybe I should go away more often."

"Don't." Her soft yet urgent order prompted a tender smile from him.

Before she could stop herself, she reached up and kissed him passionately. She smiled against his lips at his obvious surprise at her actions. His arms went around her and he kissed her back, stoking the already smoldering flames within. She hiked up her dress to her knees and straddled his lap, her mouth never losing contact with his.

Her palms rose to frame his cheeks, the soft hair of his light beard caressing her fingers, as she massaged the spots where his beautiful dimples made an appearance whenever he smiled. Their kisses had reached the incineration point when Cam pulled back slightly. Her hands moved to loosen his tie before releasing the three top buttons of his shirt.

"Angela, what are you doing?" His voice was thick with passion, and it excited her beyond reason.

"What does it feel like?"

"It feels damn good, but—"

"Don't you want me?"

"Of course I want you," he groaned as her mouth made contact with his neck. "Always."

"I want you, too," she murmured against his skin before trailing her mouth along his jaw.

"Have you changed your mind about us just being friends?"

The air was sucked from her lungs as she contemplated his question. She purposefully kept her face buried in his neck, hiding the conflicting emotions racing through her.

"We can be friends with benefits," she finally said. "Can't we?"

"Yes, we can." Hands cupped the back of her head, pulling her mouth away from his flesh. Staring deeply into her eyes, he asked, "Are you sure this is what you want?"

"I'm sure." And she was. She didn't know where this was leading, but she knew she wanted Cam right here, right now. He smiled as intent fingers unbuttoned the remainder of the buttons and spread his shirt wide. Her eyes grew huge when they encountered his muscular chest and washboard abs. "Isn't this what you want?"

"Yes." Cam's fingers reached blindly behind him for the intercom button. "Jim, take us home."

"Yes, sir."

His bared flesh was just too great a temptation for her mouth to resist. She caressed his muscled chest with lingering openmouthed kisses, enthusiastically and thoroughly tasting every inch of his exposed broad chest with her mouth, tongue and teeth.

"Mmm," she moaned appreciatively. "You must work out."

"I have a very extensive gym at home," he said around a groan.

"Keep up the good work," she whispered against his flesh. Her fingers investigated every hard, sculpted indentation in his six-pack abs. He hissed a curse when her fingers inched lower and he captured her hands with his, stilling her sensual exploration.

"Angela, you're driving me insane."

"I hope so." She kissed his neck, lingering, and tugged at her hands until he released them.

"We'll be home in about an hour." His words came out on a hiss as she raked her hard nails up his sides and then down again. "Or less...Angela." He growled her name.

"That's too long." Having made up her mind, she didn't want to wait another second. She was tired of living like a hermit. She wanted to be close to another human being. Correction, she wanted to be close to Cam. "I thought you wanted me."

"I want you anywhere and everywhere I can have you," he readily admitted, hands freely roaming up and down her bare back. "I just don't want you to have any regrets."

"I won't. I'm tired of fighting this attraction between us." She gasped as his tongue traced the outline of her ear. "We're both consenting adults who want each other. We can be together without reading more into it than that."

"I agree." He said exactly what she needed to hear to fuel her resolve to give in to their mutual desire.

"Good." She sighed in relief, which turned to a gasp when his hands squeezed her breasts softly through the thin material of her dress. "I know you've only been gone a few days, but it seemed like weeks."

"Much too long," he concurred.

He raised his head from her neck. Rapt eyes watched his fingers skim up her arms, to her shoulders, sliding under the thin straps of her gown. At her encouraging smile and nod, he slowly slid the straps down her arms, and then his hands moved to the back zipper and released it. She pulled her arms through the straps, causing her gown to pool around her waist, baring her breasts for his hungry gaze.

"You are so beautiful." His hands cupped her breasts, fingers lightly squeezing her sensitive flesh, provoking a groan of pleasure from her slightly parted lips.

"Kiss me."

Without hesitation, he sealed his mouth to hers. Her arms encircled his neck, and his took up residence on her back. They both groaned at the feel of their naked chests pressing close for the first time, and their kiss automatically kicked into high gear.

Cam's tongue unapologetically slipped between her lips and past the barrier of white teeth to slowly yet feverishly tangle with hers. She inhaled deeply and felt drunk from the smell of his woodsy cologne coupled with his unique scent, which she craved and needed to sustain her as much as she needed air and food to live. They kissed long, hard and deep, seeming unable to get enough of each other's mouths. Before things got out of hand, she forced herself to pull back and disentangle her well-kissed lips from Cam's. They were both bordering on hyperventilation.

"Do you have a condom?" She gasped the question.

He maneuvered his wallet out of his inside jacket pocket, opened it up and pulled out several foil packets. She took one from him and ripped it open.

"You came prepared." She unrolled the latex and then went to work on unfastening his pants. She smiled. "Should I be offended?"

"Absolutely not." He nipped at her lips and growled when she freed him from his restrictive pants. "It's better to have them and not need them than to need them and not have them."

"Oh really?" She chuckled at his excellent logic, and their hands battled for supremacy before successfully sheathing him together.

"Mmm-hmm. Don't you agree?"

"Yes." She arched against his unbending hardness. "I definitely do."

"Well?" His eyes twinkled in challenge.

"Well what?"

"I'm waiting." His hands caressed her hips and then pulled the gown completely from her before trailing slowly up her back, pulling her closer.

"For?" Goose bumps ran up and down her spine at his burning touch.

"For you to take advantage of me."

"Don't worry." A sultry smile turned up the corners of her mouth. "I won't disappoint you."

"I know you won't, babe."

With a quick nip at his mouth, she rose up on her knees and slowly guided him inside her by unhurried, tortuous increments until she was fully seated. They both held their breath and neither moved, enjoying the pleasure of being intimately connected. Then, at his urging, she began to move, painstakingly, slowly, torturing them both. His mouth fastened on to her breast while his hands attached to her hips, showing her what he wanted—needed—and groaning approvingly when she wholeheartedly gave it to him.

Angela felt like passing out from the exquisite pleasure quickly infusing her body. She hadn't been with a man in quite some time, but had it ever felt like this—so good that she almost couldn't bear it? So exquisite that she felt like she had died and taken up residence in heaven? So vital that she wondered how she had survived without this basic oneness for so long?

Angela's hands anchored to Cam's head, forcing his scorching mouth from her flesh until their lips were fused in a series of carnal kisses—their tongues mimicking the now-frenzied movements of their lower bodies. Her nails bit into his unyielding shoulders, and his fingers were glued to her hips as he pressed up harder and higher inside of her. Her knees sank into the soft expensive leather seat as she maneuvered for leverage, intensifying the wonderful ache of escalating pleasure inside them both.

Of course, such flawless ecstasy couldn't last forever, and much too soon the earth opened up, swallowing them into a deep abyss of spiraling passion that had them groaning in unison, grinding impossibly closer until the mercilessly intense waves of their passion crested and rapidly overflowed, leaving in its wake blissful and utter contentment.

The storm was momentarily spent, and Angela weakly collapsed against Cam as tiny yet explosive aftershocks fired through her fulfilled body. His hands gently rubbed her back, and he softly kissed her shoulder. The car effortlessly made its way down the busy street toward his house. They stayed that way for a long while, and nothing had ever felt so perfect or so right.

Chapter 9

"How was it?" Cam asked against her neck.

"You have to ask?" Her voice was breathlessly airy.

"Yeah." He lifted his head from the crook of her neck and grinned into her satisfied eyes. "Tell me."

"It was nice."

"Nice?"

She smiled at his offended tone. "It was good."

His frown increased, and her smile widened.

"Just good?"

"Okay, it was *very* good." Her laugh turned into a moan when his hands cupped her breasts, and his thumbs rubbed across her hard nipples before he took one into his hot mouth, sucking and nipping until she relented. "Okay, okay, it was great, fantastic." She clasped the back of his smooth head, holding his mouth against her tingling flesh. "Are you satisfied now?"

He released her breast to lick at her lips, then he grinned wickedly and breathed into her mouth, "Not yet, but soon."

His mouth took hers on a slow, seductive journey, expertly rekindling the temporarily cooled embers of their passion. He pulled back slightly to nibble on her lower lip, before his tongue investigated the silky skin, and then he was kissing her thoroughly again. This went on and on until they were both breathless. He ended with sweet nips at her lips, and then his mouth reluctantly released hers. Angela opened dazed eyes to stare into his and felt herself helplessly free-falling. The ability to speak had deserted her and she shivered, but not from cold.

Smiling at her gently, he picked up his tuxedo jacket and placed it around her shoulders. She shrugged it on. It was warm, inviting and smelled wonderfully of him. As if unable to resist, his mouth tasted hers again for several satisfying seconds, though he didn't allow either of them to intensify the caress. She sensed he was waiting to get her home before devouring her again.

To resist the temptation of his addictive mouth, she twisted in his arms until she reclined against his bare chest, legs stretched out on the leather seat in front of her, dreamy eyes staring out the dark, tinted limo windows, feeling safe and secure in her private little world with Cam. Another emotion was fighting to the forefront, trying to manifest itself, and she deliberately kept it corralled; she wasn't ready to go there yet. Given her horrible history with men, she honestly didn't know if she'd ever be ready to go there again.

"Are you okay?" Cam's question broke the silence.

"Yes."

"You're very quiet."

"I'm just thinking."

"About?" He kissed the top of her head, and she closed her eyes.

Part of her wanted to confide her inner turmoil to him, but she wasn't ready to bare her soul to him. Instead, she replied, "I was just thinking that this is turning out to be a very good night."

"You didn't think it would be?"

"No." She released a silent sigh of thanks that he

wasn't going to press her. He had a knack of knowing when to back off, and she appreciated that. "I didn't want to attend the ball at all. I made myself go because I was one of the organizers, and it was for charity."

"Why didn't you want to go?"

"I'm not much of a party person."

"Me, either." His arms tightened around her. "That's not true," he quickly corrected himself. "I don't mind private parties like this at all."

"This one was rather nice." A dreamy smile lit up her satisfied face. "Wasn't it?"

"What do you mean *was?* It's not over yet." His promise, spoken into her ear, sent chills of anticipation down her spine.

She half turned to smile at him. "No?"

"Not by a long shot." Their lips touched lightly, but that was enough to ignite the passion simmering just below the surface in each of them. Her palm rested against his stubbly cheek as they thoroughly refamiliarized themselves with each other's mouths for long, fulfilling seconds. "You have the sweetest mouth."

"Yours is addictive." To prove her point, she engaged in butterfly kisses with his smiling mouth.

"Yeah?"

"Yeah." She leaned in for one more spine-tingling kiss and then reclined against his chest again, pointing at the open sunroof. "Look at all of those stars. They're beautiful."

"Not as beautiful as you." She felt like purring as his strong hands insinuated themselves underneath the jacket to stroke her skin.

"I don't think I can hold a candle to them."

"They can't hold a candle to you." Her heart flipped

at his words, which seemed to be spoken from a place of truth.

"You have a wonderful gift for making me feel special."

"That's easy to do because you are special." He kissed the top of her head and then withdrew his hands from her. When she glanced questioningly at him, he said, "We're almost at my place. I guess we'd better get dressed."

"I don't want to move," she groaned in protest.

"That's fine by me." He wrapped her in his arms again and murmured into her hair, "You realize we're going to have to walk from the car to the house."

At his teasing reminder, she sat upright, returned his jacket, grabbed her dress from the floor and pulled it on. "I don't know what I was thinking." She shuddered as he ran a hand down her bare arm.

"I'm thinking I can't wait to get you home." He zipped her up and then pulled her close as his mouth gravitated toward hers. "In fact, why should I wait?"

By the time they arrived at Cam's, they were both re-dressed, though Cam had avoided her attempts to rebutton his shirt. His jacket was hooked over one finger, and his tie hung undone on either side of his neck. His disarrayed attire left little doubt as to what they had been doing in the back of the limo, but the driver's face remained impassively polite as he helped her from the car and bade them good-night.

Giggling like schoolchildren, they entered the house hand in hand. "Are you hungry?" he asked around a kiss as they stood in the foyer.

"Yes, we left before dinner."

"Complaining?"

"No, it was well worth it." She fanned herself with one hand at the memory, and he laughed.

"I'll say it was." He placed an arm around her waist and led her to the kitchen. "Come on, I can rustle us up something appetizing."

"I'll help," she offered.

He switched on the lights, and Angela's eyes took in the spacious kitchen. The room was larger than her living room. Every modern appliance occupied the cabinets. Polished stainless steel pots and pans hung suspended over a granite butcher block in the center of the room. The refrigerator, oven and dishwasher were all stainless steel. The floor was covered in gray tile, and white wooden cabinets completed the picture.

"Very nice." Angela ran her fingers across the refrigerator door. "I expected to find a personal chef in here."

"No." Cam opened the refrigerator and peered inside. "I have a cleaning lady who comes in during the week, but I do my own cooking." He turned to her. "What do you have a taste for?"

"Um…" Appreciative eyes inspected his bare chest, visible through his undone shirt. He grinned, intercepting her gaze. "Something quick."

"Quick it is. I like to eat breakfast for dinner sometimes. How about you?"

"It's my favorite dinner," she admitted.

"Omelets?"

"Perfect."

"OJ to drink, or something stronger?"

"Orange juice is fine."

He took out a pitcher and told her where to find the glasses, and she filled them before replacing the pitcher in the fridge.

"Can you get a mixing bowl out of the cabinet?" Cam nodded toward the location.

"Sure." Angela retrieved a large bowl and set it on the counter.

"Thanks, babe." Cam rewarded her with a sweet kiss. "I hate cracking eggs. I hereby delegate that job to you."

"Okay." Angela took the eggs and cracked them open before dropping them into the bowl.

Cam started grating cheese. Together they took out the remainder of the ingredients they needed to prepare their dinner. She chopped vegetables while he beat the eggs until fluffy and then added butter, sliced mushrooms and onions to two pans before placing them on the stovetop. She was working on dicing a bell pepper when he walked up behind her and wrapped his arms around her waist.

"Cam, stop it. You're going to make me cut myself," she warned him. He took the knife out of her hand and placed it on the countertop, then pulled her back against his hard length while his mouth investigated her bare shoulder and neck. "Um…Cam…"

"Hmm?" His hands slid up to cup her breasts, and his teeth worried her earlobe. At her continued silence, he asked, "What is it?"

"I…" She shook her head to clear it, trying to remember what she had been about to tell him. "Oh, that feels nice, but…the…mushrooms are going to…to burn," she managed.

"Oh. Okay." He gave her earlobe a final tug before reluctantly releasing her to tend to their dinner. He added bell pepper to the simmering veggies, and after a few minutes poured the eggs into the two frying pans. "A second longer, and I'd have had to start all over again." He effortlessly cooked both omelets simultaneously and then flipped them into plates once they were done.

"This looks great," she said, and he kissed her briefly and nodded for her to sit at the breakfast nook. She grabbed their juice, and he carried their plates over and sat down beside her.

"They're not my best. I was distracted." He ran a burning finger down her cheek. "But I think they're edible."

"Let's see." She placed a forkful of omelet in her mouth. "Mmm. Wonderful."

"Don't sound so surprised. I'm a pretty good cook, if I do say so myself."

"You are." Angela took in another mouthful of egg, chewed and swallowed before asking, "Who taught you to cook?"

"My mom. She was determined her baby wasn't going to live on take-out food." He had mimicked his mother's voice, and Angela laughed.

"You should thank her. She did a wonderful job with you." She wasn't just talking about cooking. He really was a remarkable man in so many ways.

"Thank *you*." The way he was looking at her made it very hard to breathe.

"Did you ever call her about your accident?"

She chuckled at his pained expression. "Yes, and she read me the riot act for not calling sooner." He turned his head and pointed to his ear. "Can't you see part of my ear's been chewed off?"

"Serves you right." She laughed and took a sip of her juice before returning her attention to her eggs.

"Hey, whose side are you on?"

"Yours." Her easy, truthful answer at his mock outrage elicited a wide grin from him. He leaned over, took her fork from her unresisting hand and kissed her soundly. She leaned into the kiss, hands framing his face. "What was that for?"

"Because I wanted to," he said against her clinging mouth. "Are you full?" He pulled her from her seat. They had only eaten a few bites of their food, but she was done.

"From food? Yes."

They drifted together again, and their lips met and melted effortlessly as if they were old familiar lovers. Her arms wound around his neck, and one of his arms encircled her waist while the fingers of his other hand became ensnared in her short hair, holding her mouth tight against his. Their kisses grew deep and fierce. Without releasing her mouth, he scooped her up into his arms and carried her effortlessly out of the room, down the hall and up the stairs into his bedroom.

Cam set her feet down beside the bed and released her mouth. They slowly undressed each other, carelessly tossing their clothes onto the polished red-oak floors. She sat on the edge of the bed and stared unabashedly at his magnificent body.

"Like what you see?"

"Oh yes." Appreciative eyes drank their fill of his hard physique, from his beautiful bald head to his toes and back up again. "Very much."

"You're shameless." Despite his words, an approving smile lit up his eyes.

"I'm a nurse, Mr. Stewart." She trailed her hands up his hard thighs before lying back on the bed in a seductive pose that had his eyes dilating. "The things I know about human anatomy are astounding."

"Are they now?" He lowered himself over her, holding his full weight off her with a hand placed on either side of her body. "Like what?"

"Like…" She smiled sexily, trailing her hand from his chiseled pecs to his well-defined stomach. "Maybe I should show you instead of telling you?"

"If you'd like."

"The question is—" her hand inched low on his stomach, fingers splayed wide "—would you like me to?"

"By all means." His voice was steady, but she felt his muscles contracting beneath her wandering fingers, and then he groaned deep and throaty.

"Your wish is my command." She pushed him onto his back and half covered his body with hers. Her mouth settled in the crook of his neck, and she inhaled his intoxicating cologne deeply before her tongue darted out to outline the pulse beating erratically at the base. "Want me to stop?"

"Stop? You just got started—I hope."

She laughed and slid her body down his, using her hands, lips, tongue and teeth to investigate every inch of him. She took her time, refusing to be rushed, savoring every texture and taste of him. Her tongue and then her teeth tortured his nipples, wringing a hiss of approval from him. Then his muscled chest begged for her attention, and she was happy to give it before running her tongue down and across his corrugated stomach where her fingers, lips and tongue painstakingly investigated every hard indentation.

She hummed approvingly as her mouth and hands purposefully traveled lower, encouraged and urged on by Cam's ragged moans. She nibbled across his enticing skin, enjoying his unique taste more than any food. She sweetly tortured him with butterfly kisses and lingering caresses until his hands touched the back of her head, holding her tight against his humming flesh.

"Damn, woman!" She smiled at his whispered curse and opened her mouth wider, taking more of his hot flesh into her voracious mouth. His curses turned to unintelligible groans. After a blissful eternity, his fingers anchored in her hair and pulled her skillful mouth away from his tingling flesh, and he gasped, "Enough."

"Enough?" she whispered in his ear once she crawled up his body. "But I was just warming up."

He groaned, and a pleased smile lit up her face.

"How was it?"

"The best I've ever had," he answered breathlessly. "You would have brought me to my knees if I'd been standing."

"That makes me feel all-powerful." At his intense stare, her teasing smile faltered.

"You do have power over me, Angela."

Without giving her time to contemplate or answer, he placed a hand behind her head and brought her sweet mouth to his. God, she loved kissing him. He knew exactly how to kiss her to effectively turn her into a tingling mass of need.

He took his time and thoroughly explored every treasure her mouth had to offer, and coaxed her into doing the same with him. Everything about this man was so appealing, so perfect, and for a little while at least, he was all hers.

When Cam awoke in the morning, a huge grin spread across his face as he reached across his bed in search of Angela. His face quickly fell when his seeking hand encountered only emptiness. He sat up and glanced around the room. Angela's clothes, which that had been scattered haphazardly last night, were gone, and his were neatly folded across the back of a chair.

"Angela?" He padded out of bed and went into the bathroom, but she wasn't there. "Angela?"

Damn! She was gone. But she couldn't be gone because the alarm would have sounded, and even though he slept like the dead, that blaring noise would have definitely awakened him. With his palm, he smacked his forehead. *Idiot! You forgot to set the alarm last night!* Well, he had been wonderfully preoccupied.

Scratching his chin, he glanced at the nightstand and saw the note lying there. Walking over, he picked it up and read it: *Cam, I had to be at work early this morning. You were sleeping so peacefully I didn't have the heart to wake you. I'll call you later. Angela.*

Well, that explained everything. Sighing, he picked up the phone and dialed her number. After a brief wait, she answered.

"Good morning, Cam."

"Good morning. I missed you when I woke up."

"Did you find my note?"

"Yes, but you could have woken me up. I would have driven you to work."

"I started to, but I decided to call a cab and let you sleep. You've been working so hard lately, and you looked so peaceful that I just couldn't bear to wake you." She paused. "Are you mad?"

"No, I'm not. I was just looking forward to waking up with you." He added wickedly, "I had such plans for you."

"Oh, do tell." She sounded suddenly breathless, and he could hear the excitement in her voice.

"I think I'll show you later instead," he promised. "You still owe me about twelve hours of your time."

"Oh, do I now?" She chuckled.

"Mmm-hmm, and I intend to collect every second."

"I'll be more than happy to pay up," she whispered.

"Tonight?"

"Tonight." She paused. "But I'm afraid I've got to go now. You caught me on the way to a meeting, and then I have to be in surgery."

He tsked. "You're a bigger workaholic than I am."

"It takes one to know one," she agreed. He heard background noise and envisioned her walking down a crowded hallway. "I'll see you tonight?"

"You'd better. What time do you get off?"

"Four."

"I'll pick you up at six?"

"Perfect. I'll see you then."

"Yes, you will," he said before ringing off.

Whistling a happy tune, he padded into the bathroom and started the shower. He couldn't wait until tonight.

That night, Angela met Cam at his place instead, and decided it was best to have her car since she had another early shift at the hospital in the morning. He greeted her at the door with a passionate kiss.

"Wow," she breathed when he released her mouth.

"I've been looking forward to that all day."

"I hope it didn't disappoint you."

"You never disappoint me." He led her into the living room. "Drink?"

"No, I'll wait for dinner." She smoothed fingers down the lapel of his immaculate navy suit jacket. "How was work?"

"Busy, but productive. What about you?"

"The same." She sank gratefully onto the sofa. "I love my job, but this past week has been horrific!"

"Now it's time for us to relax." Cam sat down close beside her and ran his hands down her bare arms.

"You'll get no argument from me on that."

"Good." Unable to help himself, he pulled her close again.

"You promised me dinner." Even as she protested, her body arched invitingly against his.

"I can cook something here." He nibbled on her neck.

"If we stay here, we'll never eat. We didn't begin to do justice to your wonderful omelets last night," she reminded him, kissing him quickly before pulling back. "Food first, then we can come back here for dessert."

"That sounds good, but first…" He started to kiss her again, but the doorbell rang. Sighing, he released her and stood. "Decide where you want to eat while I get rid of whoever this is."

She laughed. "Cam, be nice."

"No one's going to interrupt my night with you, babe."

Cam whistled a happy tune while walking to the door. Upon opening it, his smile froze. "Mom! What are you doing here?"

"What kind of greeting is that, Cameron?" Mabel placed a hand on her hip and smiled at him.

"I'm sorry." He gave her a long hug and a kiss on the cheek. "Of course I'm glad to see you. I'm just surprised."

"That was the idea." She laughed as he pulled her inside. "I'm relieved to see you looking fit and healthy."

Cam sighed. "Mom, I told you I was fine."

"Well, I had to see with my own two eyes in person, didn't I?" She inspected him closely and then concluded, "You look wonderful, very happy."

"I am." Cam guided her toward the living room. "Let me show you why."

"Cam, who was at the…" Angela's voice trailed off as Cam and an older woman entered the living room.

"Hello, dear, I'm Cameron's mother."

"Mrs. Stewart." Angela stood and offered her hand. "It's very nice to meet you."

"You, too…" Mabel paused and glanced at her son.

"Mom, this is Angela Brown."

"A pleasure to meet you, Angela." She smiled approvingly and turned her attention back to her son. "I didn't know you were seeing someone, Cameron."

"We're good friends, Mom." Her smile said she didn't believe that was all they were for a second. "Where are your bags? In the cab?"

"No, they're at my hotel."

"You're not staying at a hotel when I have all this room."

"Yes, I am." Mabel's stance brooked no argument. "You know I like my privacy."

"But Mom…"

"Now, you know once I've made up my mind about something, it's useless trying to make me change it." She glanced at Angela. "Besides, you don't need me hanging around underfoot when you have a nice lady friend."

"Subtle, Mom." Cam shook his head, and Angela smiled slightly.

"Subtlety is overrated," Mabel quickly returned.

"How's the family?" Cam hoped to distract her.

"Great. Everyone's wondering when you're coming for a visit."

"I'll try to swing it soon. Can I get you something to drink?"

"No, thanks, dear."

"I hope you'll be here long enough for me to plan a barbecue."

"I'd love that." Mabel's eyes lit up in anticipation. "I'm leaving on Saturday night."

"Great, I'll invite Derrick and Alesha over on Saturday and we'll make a day of it."

"That will be fun," Mabel said. "Were you two heading out?"

"We were going to dinner." Cam glanced at Angela,

who smiled and nodded in response to his unasked question. "Have you eaten, Mom?"

"No, not yet."

"Good, now you can join us."

"Please do," Angela chimed in.

"If you're sure I'm not intruding."

"Of course not." Cam stood between them and took each of their hands, ushering them outside. "I love the idea of having two beautiful ladies on my arms."

Chapter 10

A half hour later, Cam, Angela and his mother were all seated around the table at a French restaurant. Mabel and Cam did most of the talking while Angela studied the mother and son. Mabel Stewart's hair was cut short and was sprinkled with gray. She was vibrant and witty. Angela knew she had to be in her sixties, but she looked much younger. They obviously loved each other very much, and watching them, Angela realized how much she missed her own mother, who had long since died from a broken heart—among other things.

"Are you from Washington, Angela?"

Angela started at Mabel's question. "No." She managed a half smile. "South Carolina."

"Does your family still live there?"

"A few cousins and an aunt, but my parents passed away." That was halfway true—her mother had, but she had no idea where her lying father was, and she didn't care.

"I'm sorry, dear." Mabel's brown eyes filled with regret. "I didn't mean to resurrect unpleasant memories."

"It's fine." Angela forced a smile and could have kissed Cam when he covered her hand with his reassuringly and changed the subject.

"Mom, Angela's a nurse. She took care of me when I had my accident."

"Thank you for looking after him." Mabel gave her son a wry glance. "I'm sure he wasn't the best patient."

At his mother's assertion, Cam frowned and Angela hid a smile behind her hand. "What's that supposed to mean?"

"Cameron, you hate hospitals—especially when you're confined in one." Mabel turned to Angela and explained, "He had his appendix out when he was sixteen, and my Lord, the ruckus he caused was humiliating."

"Thanks for embarrassing me, Mom."

"Payback, son." Mabel chuckled, and as if to prove her point, asked, "Angela, what type of patient was my son?"

"He was…" Angela fought to suppress a smile. "He was very…" When Cam shot her a shocked glance, the smile broke through and she laughed. "I'm sorry, Cam, but you were not the best patient."

"Aha!" Mabel laughed in vindication. "Case closed." Ignoring her son's audible sigh, she continued. "He can be overbearing, but his bark is worse than his bite."

"Hello? I'm sitting right here."

His mother gave him a tolerant smile.

"I don't think he has an overbearing bone in his body," Angela said, automatically defending him.

"Really, dear?" Mabel seemed acutely interested in Angela's opinion.

"Yes." The single word was drawn out as Angela realized she had put her foot in her mouth. "He can be stubborn and tenacious, but he's also one of the kindest men I've ever met, and generous to a fault."

"See, Angela likes me."

Yes, I like you much too much.

"I can see that, dear." Mabel's smile widened. Angela

felt like she was being sized up for a wedding gown—a fact that terrified her, but thankfully Mabel's next words had nothing to do with her and Cam as a couple. "Cameron, if you talk to Derrick before I do, tell him just because he's a senator, he's not too important for me to walk into Capitol Hill and give him a piece of my mind if I don't get an invitation to see precious D.J. soon."

Cam laughed. "I'll tell him, Mom." He squeezed Angela's hand. "Angela is Alesha's best friend."

"Oh, how nice. Isn't D.J. the cutest thing you've ever seen?" Angela nodded in agreement and sighed visibly in relief at the change to a safer topic—or so she thought, until Mabel glanced pointedly at Cam and bemoaned, "I've been waiting forever on a grandchild from this one."

Cam placed a hand to his head as if in pain. "Oh, Mom, please not that again."

"Well, you're not getting any younger, Cameron."

"I'm only thirty-seven." He took a sip of his drink and professed, "I'm in my prime."

"Your prime?" Mabel chuckled. "Cameron, you're—"

"Mrs. Stewart," Angela interrupted, hoping to spare Cam and herself further talk of grandchildren. "Cam and I are D.J.'s godparents."

"Is that how you two met?"

Angela opened her mouth to answer, but Cam beat her to it. "No, actually we met at Derrick and Alesha's wedding."

"You've been dating all this time?" Mabel glanced from one to the other. "Why haven't you mentioned Angela before now, Cameron?"

"We just recently started dating, Mom."

"Oh, I see." Mabel nodded and then turned her attention to Angela. "You, Alesha and I must do lunch while I'm in town."

"I'd like that, Mrs. Stewart."

"Call me Mabel, dear." She glanced at Cam and then back to her. "I have a feeling that if my son has a say in things, I'll be seeing much more of you, so let's not stand on formalities."

Cam sighed and shook his head tolerantly. Angela managed a smile and willed the nervous butterflies taking up residence in her stomach to settle down with all this talk about babies and commitment.

Several hours later, Cam and Angela returned to his house after dropping Mabel off at her hotel. Angela felt Cam's eyes on her as she walked slowly into the living room.

"I'm sorry if you were uncomfortable at dinner."

At his words, she turned to face him. "I wasn't," she said quickly. At his dubious stare she conceded, "Maybe a little, but I had a good time."

"Did you?"

"Yes, your mother's very nice." And that was the truth. She liked Mabel.

"Even though she's an unrepentant matchmaker?" Cam's smile coaxed one out of her.

"What mother isn't?"

"I love her dearly, but I'm her only child and she can't help taking great interest in my personal life, much to my dismay."

"Well, that's to be expected." She tried to appear natural, but Cam must have seen the trepidation bubbling just beneath the surface.

"Angela." Cam eliminated the distance between them and took her hands in his. "Nothing has changed between us."

"Hasn't it?" She hoped that simple question didn't make her sound as terrified as she felt at the moment.

"No. We're friends—good friends." She was relieved by his answer, but she wondered if he really meant it—or more importantly, if she really believed it anymore.

She was an independent career woman who had no intention of losing her identity personally or professionally because of a man. She was not going to be ensnared in an emotional roller-coaster ride no matter how much she liked Cam—and she did like him very much. She *wasn't* going down that booby-trapped commitment road again, not for anything or anyone. She couldn't.

"I should be going."

His fingers tightened in hers, halting her exit. Cam's expression was downright sinful as he asked, "Don't you want dessert?"

This crazy yearning for him—to simply be in his presence—was getting out of hand, and she knew it. She also knew she should walk straight out the door, but her feet refused to move. His decadent expression sent tremors of desire racing up and down her spine, and instead of leaving like she knew she should, she wound her arms around his neck.

"What do you have that I might be interested in?"

His answer was to kiss her softly. "A lot more of this." He sighed into her mouth.

She closed her eyes as they kissed, and felt as if she was floating, like a feather being lifted and tossed about by a caressing wind. When she opened her eyes, the look in his nearly caused her to close hers again. She had never had a man look at her so adoringly—as if his only purpose on this earth was to please her.

Before she could say anything, he took her mouth again in a scorching kiss that went on and on, melting her from the inside out. She didn't remember walking up the stairs, but she must have, or Cam carried her, because now they were in his bedroom.

He undressed her leisurely, and she did the same to him. Soon they were lying on the bed. Cam pulled Angela on top and ran his hands down the length of her again and again as their mouths feasted until she thought she would succumb to a deadly case of pleasure overload. Their limbs entangled, and they arched and pulled closer, giving and receiving all each had to give.

My God, he destroyed her with gentle, unhurried kisses and caresses. When her hands and body tried to rush him, he was having none of it, refusing to deviate from his slow, thorough possession that was nothing short of masterful. He touched, tasted and caressed every inch of her until she was strung tighter than a bowstring, hoping he would never stop touching her. He played her flesh expertly and she melted into him, was absorbed by him, until her entire body quivered with uncontrollable need. Her mind was filled only with thoughts of him, and her heart was perilously close to letting him invade every part of her soul.

They were silent except for the satisfied sighs and groans that erupted from them as they pleased and were pleasured. Then they were flying, soaring high above the clouds, hoisted by their intense passion. When the tumult inevitably reached its unbearable precipice, they jumped over into madness together, holding tight before finally letting go.

A while later, Angela lay on her side with Cam snuggled close against her back. She was blissfully content, and her body still resonated from the intimate imprint of his and the numbing aftereffects of their recent lovemaking. For this second, she was happy and content. Then the phone rang, disturbing the peace and quiet. Angela eventually stirred once she realized it was hers.

"Don't answer it," Cam softly ordered when she turned to face him, regret shining in her eyes.

"I have to." She recognized that ring tone. "It's the hospital." He sighed, reached over and handed her the phone. She smiled her thanks and sat up, resting against the pillows. "Hello." She listened and tensed. "How bad? How many are we expecting? Okay, I'm in Maryland, but I can be there in about an hour—maybe a little less." She sat completely upright, holding the sheet against her breasts with one hand. "Yes, all right. I'm on my way."

"Trouble?" Cam ran a hand down her tense back.

"There's been a bad accident, and they're calling in personnel to handle the overflow." She touched his cheek before getting out of bed. "I'm sorry."

"Don't be sorry. It's your job."

"Thanks for understanding." She kissed him softly before getting out of bed. "It's a good thing I met you here and have my car."

"Yeah." He got up, grabbed her and pulled her into an embrace.

"Can I use your shower?"

"Of course, but first…" He kissed her until she didn't know where she ended and he began, until she wanted nothing more than to forget about everything except the two of them.

"I have to go." She pressed against his chest while running her tongue over her lower lip. "I wish I didn't, but I have to."

"I know." He grinned as if a pleasing thought was forming in his mind. "Why don't I join you in the shower?"

"I don't think that's a good idea, Cam." The wicked

gleam in his eyes made her smile. "I need to hurry, and you will definitely slow me down."

"I'll be good."

"Oh, will you?" She backed away from him and the great temptation he embodied.

"I promise."

He grabbed her hand and pulled her into the bathroom that was larger than her living room. He turned on the multihead shower and pulled her underneath the warm cascade of water. Before she could protest—not that she was going to protest—his mouth captured hers. She had to admit that he was pretty good, only prolonging her shower by a few wonderfully steamy minutes.

After she had dressed, he walked her to the door and kissed her goodbye. As she got into her car and drove away, she glanced in the rearview mirror, watching Cam wave goodbye. She wondered why it felt so wrong to be leaving a man she had promised herself not to become attached to. Of course, she knew the disturbing answer to that question. What she didn't know was what she was going to do about it.

Angela groaned and buried her head deeper into the pillow, trying to drown out the irritating ring of her phone. Who in the name of God was calling her at—she glanced at the clock with one eye—eight o'clock in the morning after the longest and busiest night of her life? Okay, a normal person would be up and dressed by now, but she had just finished what was virtually a grueling double shift, having left the hospital only a few hours ago. All she wanted was to sleep the rest of the day away. Was that too much to ask?

Still lying on her stomach with her face buried in her pillow, her hand reached blindly in the direction of the noisy instrument and yanked it up, bringing it to her ear. "Hello?"

"Hi, babe."

"Cam?" She rolled over onto her back and tried to focus. "Hi."

"I woke you. Didn't I?" He sounded apologetic, and she didn't have the heart to confirm his fears.

"No, no, I was awake."

"Really?" He sounded skeptical, and she couldn't help smiling.

"Well, almost." She hid a yawn behind one hand and tried to sound more alive when she asked, "What's up?"

"I have a surprise for you."

"A surprise?" She pushed her wayward bangs out of her sleepy eyes. "What is it?"

"You'll find out later. I called the hospital, and they said you're off today."

"Yes, thank God!"

He laughed at her exuberant response. "Are you going to be home around noon?"

"Yes, and in bed," she groaned, giving up all pretense of being fit for conversation. "I'm so tired."

"Poor baby." His soothing, sympathetic voice enveloped her like a warm, soft cocoon. "What I have planned will pick you right up."

"That's a tall task today." She turned on her side and snuggled deeper into the welcoming softness of her down pillow. "I don't think anything can revive me except about eight more hours of sleep."

"I hope you'll settle for four," he mysteriously counteroffered. "Go back to sleep, and your surprise will be there at noon."

"'Kay. Bye."

"Bye, baby." He chuckled softly. "Sleep tight."

The phone slipped from her fingers, and she immediately fell unconscious. The only thing that woke her up four hours later was the incessant ringing of the doorbell. Poking her head out from under the pillow, she groaned as the annoying doorbell continued to pierce the blessed quiet. Who on earth was at her door? She vaguely remembered a phone call from Cam stating something was happening at noon—or had that been a dream?

Sliding listlessly out of bed and placing on a robe, she padded from the bedroom and nearly collided with a wall but made it to the front door in one piece. Lord, she hoped it wasn't Cam on the other side, or he'd get the shock of his life. She hadn't bothered to glance in a mirror, but she could imagine how she looked, and it wasn't pretty.

She glanced through the peephole and balked. A uniformed limo driver stood waiting patiently for her to answer. *Oh, Cam, what have you done?* Belting her robe tighter, she cracked open the door and peered out.

"Yes?"

"Ms. Angela Brown?"

"Yes, that's me."

"Mr. Stewart sent me. I'm Ron, and I'll be your driver for today."

"Driver?" She blinked the sleep from her eyes. "For what?"

"I'm not at liberty to say, ma'am." Ron smiled. "But you do have an appointment at one." He eyed her robe. "May I suggest you get dressed so we won't be late?"

"I'm sorry, I should have been ready, but—"

"Don't worry, ma'am," he interrupted politely. "I'll wait in the car. Just come out when you're ready."

"Okay. Thanks." She closed the door and headed back to her bedroom.

She started to call Cam and ask what he had planned,

but she knew he wouldn't tell her. Shrugging, she returned to her bedroom, glanced regretfully at her welcoming bed, then bypassed it and went into the bathroom to get ready for her secret day.

Twenty minutes later, she was being helped into the back of the luxurious black limo on her way to her surprise. She felt like a movie star as she sank into the soft leather seat and glanced out of the dark tinted windows as the car effortlessly weaved through traffic.

Her eyes grew to twice their normal size when a half hour later, the car stopped outside of the Olympus Spa, a full-service health resort that rivaled any of its Beverly Hills counterparts. She had been longing to try it, but a simple facial cost more than a week's salary. Cam must be spending a fortune on this.

When the door was unlocked by the driver, she opened her mouth to tell him to take her back home, but instead took his hand as he helped her out of the car. She couldn't disappoint Cam by not accepting his gift. Besides, she was dying to see what this place was like on the inside and if the service here was as good as she had read about.

"Ms. Brown?" A smiling woman dressed in a pink smock approached as soon as she entered the spa.

"Yes." She fought to keep her mouth from gaping open as she beheld the opulent interior—marble floors, hand-painted murals of nature occupying some of the pristine white walls and sparkling crystal chandeliers hanging proudly from the high-vaulted ceiling.

"I'm Cynthia. Mr. Stewart has planned a marvelous day for you," Cynthia said while ushering Angela quickly down the hallway into a large private room, at the center of which was a massage table. "We'll start with a full-body herbal massage. If you'll get undressed, the masseuse will be with you in about ten minutes, and if there's anything you require, please don't hesitate to ask. We want your day with us to be outstanding."

"Thank you very much," Angela mumbled, and was rewarded by a smile before being left alone.

Angela did as requested, undressed and lay face down on the heavenly padded and warm massage table with only a white fluffy towel covering her. She had no sooner gotten settled than the door opened, admitting a pleasant-looking woman who introduced herself as Celeste. What followed was the most heavenly, relaxing massage she had ever received, during which Celeste used different, wonderful-smelling herbs on every part of her body.

The pleasure didn't stop with the massage. From there she was treated to a facial, and then whisked away for a body wrap that she never wanted to end, and finished with another amazing massage. She then had an amazing aromatherapy session, followed by a first-rate lunch. A manicure and pedicure were next, and finally, at five o'clock, she had her hair done. She had the most wonderful, relaxing day ever.

When she got home that evening, she showered, changed into a sleeveless red cocktail dress and quickly left again. As she drove in her own car, she thought how spoiled she had gotten because she wished her limo driver was still chauffeuring her around. She laughed out loud. Cam, it seemed, was creating a pampered diva.

Angela arrived at Cam's and rang the doorbell. When he answered, she flew into his arms without speaking and pressed her mouth to his. His strong arms encircled her waist, and he picked her up so that her feet were dangling in midair as their mouths fought for supremacy.

"Well, hello, beautiful." He released her mouth and lowered her feet to the ground, pulling her inside. "Did you enjoy your day?"

"Oh yes!" She wound her arms tighter around his neck. "It was wonderful, but you shouldn't have done it. I'm sure it was much too expensive."

"What have I told you about accepting a gift?" She smiled at his exasperated expression and looked appropriately chastised. "Everyone treated you well?"

"Like royalty," she assured him. "Thank you so much for arranging it for me."

"You're welcome." His hands ran up and down her back. "You deserved a little pampering."

"I don't know if I deserved it, but I certainly needed it." She tilted her head thoughtfully and asked, "Why are you so good to me?"

"Because nothing gives me more pleasure." His words caused her heart to skip a beat. This man was simply too good to be true, and he was hers—for the time being, she forced herself to amend. "You always look fabulous, but today you're absolutely glowing."

"Thanks to you and the spa." She sighed happily at the memory. "They did things to my body that are beyond description."

"Better than I do?" Her fingers smoothed the frown from his mouth, and she kissed his lips softly.

"Baby, nobody is better than you." Her fingers caressed his lightly hair-covered jaw.

"Really?" His eyes lit up, and she could tell her assertion pleased him.

"Really." Unable to help herself, she pressed her mouth to his again for long seconds, only pulling back to ask, "Let me make you dinner?"

"Nope." He shook his head. "This is your day and night to relax. I'll take you out."

"I thought you'd say that. If you won't let me cook dinner for you—" she switched to her backup plan "—then

I insist you let me take you out to thank you properly for my wonderful day."

"If you really want to thank me—" his mouth captured hers again, quick and hard "—I know the perfect way."

"Cam, behave." She pushed out of his arms, trying to return her heart rate to normal. "You're always doing things for me. I want to do this for you." She gave him a smile designed to melt any resistance. "Please."

"Okay," he relented, as she had hoped he would. "Where are we going?"

"That's for me to know," she said, fighting a groan when his arm encircled her waist and pulled her close again.

"And me to find out?"

"Yep."

"How about a hint."

"No chance."

"I bet I could coerce it out of you." His mouth played with hers.

"You definitely could." She pressed closer to him and whispered, "But I'd be disappointed if you did."

"Okay." He appeared to give in, and glanced down at his jeans and then at her red dress. "Give me a few minutes to change."

"You can have all the time you need."

He grinned. "Wanna help me?"

"I'd love to, but if I did, we'd never make it out of the bedroom and you know it."

He cocked an eyebrow. "And that would be a bad thing?"

"No, it wouldn't, but it would ruin my surprise."

"Okay, I don't want to do that." He paused and added, "You can't blame a guy for trying."

"You can try again later," she promised, and shivers

raced up and down her spine as he growled appreciatively. "But for now, go change." Before her resolve crumbled, she gave him a gentle shove toward the stairs.

"How should I dress? A suit?"

She chewed her lower lip thoughtfully. "I think a nice sports coat and slacks will suffice."

"I'll be back in a flash." He treated her to that gorgeous dimpled smile of his before ascending the stairs two at a time.

Those ever-present warning bells were going off in her head again, signaling that she was beginning to care too much about him. The dreamy expression on her face slowly fell away as she watched him disappear around a corner. She silently tried to convince herself that she simply wanted to thank a *friend* for being extraordinarily nice and generous to her.

She failed miserably in that endeavor.

Chapter 11

To start things off, Angela treated Cam to dinner at his favorite steak house. Next, they arrived at Bennie's Jazz Club, and she was thrilled when Cam's eyes lit up in happy surprise, informing her she had made the right choice.

"First the steak house and now this." Cam glanced fondly around the medium-sized club with its low, intimate lighting and cozy, well-dispersed seating comprised of booths and tables. "This is one of my favorite places."

"I know." She smiled as they were shown to a secluded booth to the right of the stage.

"How do you know?"

"I wanted to do something special to thank you for my wonderful day, and just in case you refused my invitation to cook for you, I called Alesha and Derrick to find out where we should go, and here we are."

He grinned. "You know you're going to get their tongues wagging more than they already are about us, don't you?"

"I know, but I needed some input." Angela had already endured merciless teasing from Alesha, but she had wanted to do this for Cam. She refused to allow herself to dwell on why pleasing him was so important to her.

"Well, remind me to thank them on Saturday."

"I will." She snuggled close to his side as the band took the stage and began playing. They were silent and enjoyed the music for a few minutes before she asked, "Are you having a good time?"

"No." He smiled at her. "I'm having a great time."

"Good." She ran her hand up his hard thigh and grinned when he groaned. "But save your strength, because the night's far from over."

"I can't wait to see what comes next," he growled into her ear, pulling her closer to his side.

"Ladies and gentlemen, I just spotted an old friend in the audience," one of the band members was saying. "Cam, get up here and let's see if you still remember how to play."

Angela's eyes widened and she glanced at Cam, who smiled and waved his hand but made no move to go up on stage. "You play?"

"Just for fun," Cam admitted. "I haven't done it in a long time."

"Come on, Cam, don't keep us waiting," the band member continued cajoling him onto the stage.

"Go on, I'd love to hear you play."

"I don't want to ruin our evening."

"Ruin it? If you play half as good as you sing, I'm in for a treat." She was rewarded for her words with a grin. "Go on," she urged again.

"Don't make me come down there and get you, Cam," the man with the microphone threatened, and received laughs in return from the audience, many of whose eyes were glued on Cam and Angela.

"All right, James." Cam finally stood. "I'm coming."

"Well, come on, then." James laughed as Cam approached the stage. "Ladies and gents, you're in for a treat now."

Cam shook his head at James as he walked onto the stage, exchanging handshakes and hugs with the six band members before taking a seat behind the piano. After talking with the group for a few seconds, they started to play. Cam played three songs with them and had a lengthy solo in one song, which had Angela's jaw dropping in amazement. He was fantastic! She didn't know why she was surprised. He was top-notch at everything he did.

Of course, in standard Cam fashion, he did something that completely threw her for a loop. He dedicated Erroll Garner's jazz hit "Misty" to her. He stared directly into her appropriately misty eyes while he played, and everyone except the two of them disappeared from the room at that point. Angela was lost in Cam's expressive eyes and hypnotized by the sweet, seductive music he played just for her.

When he finished the song, Cam left the stage to applause and pats on the back. When he returned to the table and sat beside Angela again, she was valiantly fighting back tears.

"You were incredible," she said as he took a gulp of his drink. "I've seen the piano at your house, but I had no idea you played."

"Yeah, Mom insisted I take piano lessons growing up." He screwed up his face in distaste and she laughed, glad she had a handle on her threatening tears. "I hated them back then, but I have to admit I learned to love the instrument later in life—but don't tell her I said that."

"I won't." Angela winked conspiratorially. "You're just full of surprises, aren't you?"

"Babe, you don't know the half of it—" he paused and purposefully added "—yet."

"Mmm." She brought her mouth within centimeters

of his. "I'm looking forward to finding out more, Mr. Stewart."

"And I'm so looking forward to enlightening you, babe." They kissed briefly and unsatisfactorily before sitting back, but they remained close.

The look he gave her could have sparked a forest fire.

Without removing her eyes from his, she picked up her nonalcoholic strawberry daiquiri, hoping the coolness of the drink would douse the flames of desire licking through her body. Cam's grin widened as if aware of her aroused state, and he draped an arm behind her.

"How did you like my solo?"

Her eyes grew dreamy at his whispered reminder of the highlight of the evening, as far as she was concerned. "It was my favorite part of your performance."

"It was just for you." He gazed into her overwhelmed eyes and softly questioned, "Do you feel the way I do about us—that nothing and no one else matters?"

She was too full of emotion to speak, and he smiled at her tenderly, pulled her close to his side and thankfully allowed his question to go unanswered.

They stayed at the club for a few more hours, enjoying the music and being with each other. All of the acts were really good, but Angela didn't enjoy any of them as much as Cam playing with the band.

"As fantastic as this evening has been..." Cam whispered in her ear during an intermission, sending shivers dancing up and down her spine.

"Yes?" She glanced up into his burning, seductive eyes.

"Why don't we take this party back to my place?"

"That is an excellent idea." At her acquiescence, he took her hand and led her out.

When they arrived back at his house, they were kissing

and laughing because he was trying to unlock the door, and she wouldn't release his mouth so that he could see what he was doing.

Finally, the lock gave way and they fell into the entryway, slamming the door behind them. They kissed and danced their way to the bedroom, shedding clothes along the way, creating a trail. Once they reached their destination, they fell onto the bed in a tangled mass of clinging arms and legs, clothed only in underwear.

"You were going to show me a few more surprises." Angela spoke against his mouth. "Remember?"

"Think you can handle them?" Cam took her earlobe between his teeth while deft fingers unhooked her bra.

"Try me," she groaned as his hands cupped her breasts and his teeth took love bites out of her neck.

"You asked for it." Raising his head, he smiled into her passion-glazed eyes and nipped at her lower lip before promising, "I'm going to show you the remarkable things I can do with just my tongue."

Her eyes widened, and her heart somersaulted in her chest. He grinned wickedly and started a thorough, mind-blowing exploration that had her writhing in ecstasy as he painstakingly moved from her head to her toes until she thought she would die from the exquisite pleasure he tortured her with—until they went insane together.

Oh, God, did he ever have a talented tongue!

Angela made it home from work, showered and dressed in jeans and a T-shirt. She was cooking dinner for Cam tonight. Before she could begin cooking, the doorbell rang.

"Cam, hi." She greeted him gaily. He seemed a little tense, like something was on his mind. "You're right on time."

"Hi, gorgeous." He gave her a quick kiss and handed her a bouquet of lilacs.

"How pretty." She smiled at the flowers. "Thank you."

"You're welcome." He stared at her as if he wanted to say something but didn't know how.

"Is something wrong?"

"No."

"Well, have a seat in the living room while I put these in water." His hand halted her exit, and she glanced at him questioningly. "What?"

"Can we talk first?"

"Sure." She preceded him into the living room and sat beside him on the sofa, placing her flowers on the coffee table. "What is it?"

"I have a great time with you, Angela."

"I enjoy being with you, too."

"Yeah?"

"Yes."

"Good, because I want us to be exclusive." He came to the point. She grew a little uncomfortable under his penetrating stare.

"I'm not seeing anyone else," she slowly assured him.

"But?"

"Let's just enjoy being together without reading too much into things."

"Meaning?"

"We enjoy each other's company, so why can't we just keep things as they are?"

"For how long?" When she didn't respond, he took one of her hands in his. "Babe, I know why you're hesitant to commit. You've been hurt in the past, but I'm simply asking that you give us a chance and don't penalize me for the way other jerks have treated you. Is that too much to ask?"

It was a very logical thing to ask, but she didn't know if she could do it. When she remained silent, he asked, "Angela?"

"Cam, I don't want to hurt you." That was the truth, and she didn't want to be hurt, either. "I've been honest from the beginning when I told you I'm not looking for a serious relationship."

"Yes, you were," he agreed quietly.

"I thought we were enjoying being together without any strings attached. You said you were fine with that. Has that changed?"

"I know what I said."

"But?"

"But we have a great time together, and I know you feel the connection between us. I hoped you'd changed your mind about letting me in." He paused and asked hopefully, "Will you let me in?"

"As much as I've ever let anyone, you are in," she confessed.

"Am I? Really? Or are you holding me at arm's length?" She met his unflinching gaze and shrugged her shoulders helplessly.

"It's hard to get over being hurt, Cam."

"I know." He rubbed her arms, and his compassionate gaze was almost her undoing. "Let me help you."

"Let's just take it slow and see what happens." She knew that wasn't what he wanted to hear, but it was the best she was able to offer, and frankly, that little bit scared her to death.

"Okay," he relented, pulling her close. She sighed in relief.

"I was about to start cooking dinner." She pulled back and smiled into his guarded eyes. "Want to join me?" She thought he was going to refuse when he continued staring at her as if trying to figure out what to do.

"Sure," he finally answered, smiling slightly.

"Good." She grabbed his hand and pulled him behind her. "You can chop the vegetables."

"I'm an excellent chopper."

His now-teasing tone cajoled a chuckle from her. "One of your many talents, huh?"

"One of them," he agreed.

When they entered the kitchen, she motioned to the chopping board while she pulled fish out of the refrigerator and started to season it. Suddenly her hand was grasped, and she was pulled into Cam's arms while his mouth simultaneously captured hers. This kiss was nothing like the one they had shared a few moments ago. This time he kissed her as if he were branding her as his, sucking all breath from her lungs and imprinting his lips onto hers while his tongue passionately stroked, teased and conquered until her knees were weak and she felt ready to faint.

"Just so you know, I'm not giving up on you, babe," he whispered against her mouth before releasing her.

She reached behind her and grabbed the counter to keep from falling to the ground in an undignified heap, and stared at his back when he started chopping the vegetables. She placed a hand to her thoroughly kissed mouth and continued to stare at him until he turned, gave her a grin and then turned back to his task.

Jesus! This man never did what she expected, and he was a master of keeping her off balance. Cam seemed more than willing to bide his time with her and methodically wear her down. She had to admit, he was doing an excellent job of it, and she honestly didn't know how much longer she could continue clinging to the insane notion that they were just friends. She also had no idea how she was going to stop her contrary heart from lying down at his feet in absolute surrender.

Cam sipped his iced tea as he sat across the table from Derrick. This was just what he needed, some time with his boy to relax and unwind.

"By the way," Cam began as he and Derrick waited for their lunch to be served. "Mom's in town, and she told me to inform you she wants to see D.J. and Alesha soon. I'm having a barbecue for her Saturday, and you're all required to be there."

"We'll be there, and I know she's in town." At Cam's surprised expression he explained, "She came by the house last night to see us and…" Derrick trailed off with a wide grin.

Cam warily asked, "And what?"

"And to talk about you and Angela." Derrick's grin widened at Cam's horrified expression.

"Please tell me you and my mother weren't discussing my sex life."

"Hey, man, Mama Mabel brought it up."

"Just shoot me now." Cam dropped his head in his hands. Derrick's hoot of laughter echoed in the room, causing several curious glances to be thrown their way.

"When did you introduce her to Angela?"

"We all went to dinner a few nights ago when she got into town. It was nice, but Angela was a little uncomfortable."

"Any woman would be, meeting your mother."

Cam shrugged. "It was just dinner."

"With your mother," Derrick stressed.

"Well, I didn't plan it. She just showed up, and I had to

invite her or she would have tanned my hide in front of Angela." Derrick laughed heartily, and Cam joined him.

"She wants a grandbaby." Derrick barely got the sentence out through his laughter.

"Well, she has one. Or one who's like a grandchild to her, at any rate," Cam indignantly reminded him.

"And she loves him, but she wants a grandbaby from *you*."

"What about what I want?" Cam scowled darkly.

"Hey, don't kill the messenger." Derrick held up his hands.

"You're just enjoying this far too much," Cam accused his friend.

"I am," Derrick readily agreed. "It's your payback for all the unsolicited advice you've given me over the years."

Cam cocked an eyebrow at him. "And how did that advice turn out for you, Senator?"

"Great," Derrick admitted around a chuckle. "Mama Mabel just wants you to be happy, Cam. We all do."

"I am happy, thank you very much, and I'll deal with my relationship with Angela in my own way." Cam took a needed sip of his drink. "If Mom thinks I'm going to bow to her whims, she's got another think coming."

"Hey, man, stop fighting it. She's going to get what she wants sooner or later, and you know it." Derrick leaned back while the waiter placed their lunches on the table. "Really Cam, I don't see the problem. You and Mama Mabel both want the same thing."

"I can't let her *know* I want what she wants." Cam stared at his friend in exasperation. "I'd never live that down."

"Oh brother!" Derrick raised his eyes heavenward and then asked, "So, how are things going with you and Angela?"

"Pretty good."

Derrick frowned. "Only *pretty good?*"

"Yeah." Cam sighed heavily and elaborated, "She's really afraid of commitment—I mean, to the point of being terrified by it. Even though we've slept together, she insists on clinging to the insane notion that we're just *friends.*"

Derrick placed his fork down and sat forward at Cam's admission. "So you two have…"

"Yes." Cam grinned. "Several times."

"Well, well, well," Derrick drawled, grinning at him like an idiot.

"Oh, stop it!" Cam shook his head and chuckled at his best friend. "You're worse than a teenage girl."

"Just enjoying watching your downfall, my friend," Derrick teased.

"Shut up and eat!" Cam chuckled.

A bright and sunshiny Saturday dawned. The high temperature was forecast to be in the low seventies. It was perfect cookout weather. Cam's backyard was a bee-hive of activity. Angela, Cam, Mabel, Alesha, Derrick and D.J. were seated on benches around a table on the glassed-in patio, for D.J.'s sake.

Angela occupied a padded bench, smiling down at D.J. while he lay in her arms, nearly asleep. She didn't give it a second thought when Cam straddled the bench behind her, sitting until he was pressed against her back. He reached over her shoulder to touch D.J.'s tiny hand.

"You're very good with him, dear." Angela looked up as Mabel smiled at her before glancing whimsically at her son. "Maybe one day…" Mabel's words trailed off.

Cam sighed, and Derrick, who was sitting beside Ale-sha, hid a laugh behind his hand.

"Um, thank you." Angela smiled nervously, suddenly feeling that without her knowledge, she had been auditioning for Mabel's secret casting call for a daughter-in-law. "He's such a good baby."

"He is, even though at times he has his father's temperament," Alesha chimed in.

"Hey, what is that supposed to mean?" Derrick asked with fake indignation.

"Nothing, baby." Alesha kissed his frowning mouth. "I just mean that he's definitely your son."

"Well, he'd better be," Derrick said, and they all laughed.

"You'll make a wonderful mother, dear," Mabel predicted, her attention still trained on Angela. "Have you ever thought about settling down?"

"Well... I..." Angela swallowed hard.

"Oh, Mom." Cam sighed, and though Angela couldn't see his face, she could tell from his voice that he was smiling tolerantly. "Please leave Angela alone."

Mabel glanced innocently from Angela to her son. "What did I do?"

"That's a rhetorical question, right?" Cam chuckled.

"Let me put him down, Angie." Alesha thankfully interrupted what Angela feared would turn into a more awkward conversation than it already was. Angela relinquished a now-sleeping D.J. to his mom. "Why don't you come with me?"

"I'd love to." Angela stood, thankful for the opportunity to escape, and followed Alesha into the house. "Thanks for the save," she whispered to Alesha as they walked away.

"Anytime." Alesha smiled. "Mabel does seem determined for you and Cam to make a commitment."

"No kidding?"

"Well, you can't blame her. You and Cam are good together."

"Alesha…"

"I'm not saying another word." Alesha laid D.J. down in his crib. "I think you've been traumatized enough for one day."

"True," Angela agreed with a slight smile. "And thank you."

"Don't mention it." Alesha waited until they had exited the room before adding teasingly, "You know, if you need any help planning your wedding…"

"Argh! You promised not another word," Angela exclaimed, placing both hands to her head as if she was in pain. "I'm going to check on things in the kitchen."

"Okay, I'm sure Mabel will want to discuss china patterns with me." Angela gave her friend a stern look, and Alesha held up her hands in defense. "Just kidding—sort of." Alesha winked before retreating in the opposite direction, trailing tinkling laughter.

Angela glanced heavenward and prayed, "Save me from matchmaking friends."

Chapter 12

Angela stopped by the kitchen to check on the food simmering on the stovetop and to take a few more minutes to compose herself before rejoining the group. She was halfway into the room before she spotted Mabel removing some eggs from the refrigerator. Well, at least she wasn't outside discussing china patterns with Alesha. That was a definite plus.

"Is D.J. settled in?" Mabel asked without turning around.

"Yes." Angela took a breath and entered the kitchen. "That little darling is out like a light."

"Children can be such a joy," Mabel said.

"Yes, they can."

"I'm glad we have a moment alone." Mabel turned to face her. "I hope I didn't embarrass you earlier, dear."

"No, of course not." Angela smiled as she told the tiny lie.

"Are you sure?" At Angela's nod, she chuckled and said, "I'm glad. I had to escape into the house because Cameron turned on music and insists on singing along."

Angela heaved a silent sigh of relief at the change in subjects and laughed at Mabel's distasteful expression. "He has a wonderful voice. Don't you think?"

"You've heard him sing?"

"Yes, we went out to a karaoke bar." Angela grinned at the happy memory. "He brought the house down."

"I see he's still living out his rock-star fantasy." Mabel chuckled, and Angela smiled widely when Mabel shook her head as if she didn't know what to do with her wayward son. "He has always loved music, though I had to practically threaten him to get him to take piano lessons."

"He played with a jazz band when we went out the other night." Angela smiled at the memory. "He's quite musically inclined."

"Well, it seems like you two have really been spending a lot of quality time together," Mabel said.

"We're friends, and we have a good time together," Angela slowly admitted before turning to the stove to lift the lid off a pot.

"Anyone watching you two can see that." Mabel gave an approving nod. "I'm glad he's dating you."

"Thank you." Angela took longer than necessary to stir the baked beans before replacing the lid and turned to find Mabel frowning as she opened one cabinet door and then another. "What are you looking for, Mabel?"

"The large mixing bowl." Mabel sighed and then laughed. "Every time I come for a visit, Cameron has rearranged this kitchen. I swear he does it just to annoy me."

"It's in here." Angela walked over, opened a cabinet and pulled out a steel bowl. "Will this do?"

"Perfect!" Mabel took the bowl with a smile. "You seem to know your way around this kitchen."

"Well, Cam and I cooked together once."

"Just once?" Mabel placed four sticks of butter in the bowl.

"Yes, he made me breakfast."

"Really?" At Mabel's wide grin, Angela realized her mistake.

"It wasn't really breakfast…I mean, it was, but it wasn't in the morning. We were both hungry one night and he just…" She trailed off, unsure if her rambling explanation was hurting or helping her.

"Just what, dear?" Mabel's eyes lit with curiosity.

"What are you making?" Angela hoped to divert her from the current uncomfortable topic.

"Pound cake." Thankfully, Mabel seemed willing to let her off the hook, at least for now.

"My mother made a wonderful pound cake. I always wanted the recipe, but…" Angela's voice trailed off sadly, and Mable touched her hand.

"I'll give you mine before I leave."

"I'd like that."

"In fact, why don't you come and help me with this one?" Without waiting for a response, Mabel took her hand and led her over to the bowl. "You mix, and I'll add ingredients."

"Okay." Angela turned on the mixer as Mabel began adding ingredients.

"We start by creaming a pound of room-temperature butter, and then we add two-and-a-half to three cups of sugar until smooth. If I add dried fruit or nuts, I add less sugar. Then we add six eggs, one at a time, blending each one well." She chuckled at Angela's widened eyes. "I know the ingredients are sinful, but we old folks believe in cooking with love, not counting calories."

"Nothing tastes as good as your wonderful traditional, recipes, either." Angela smiled. "As a nurse, I know I should be more health conscious, but Cam can tell you that I love rich-tasting food."

"We all need to indulge once in a while."

"I agree."

"I like to add butter and lemon flavoring, more lemon than butter though." Mabel poured some of each extract into the bowl without measuring.

"I see you don't measure, either."

"Sometimes I do, but it's all about what looks, smells and tastes right." Mabel replaced the bottles on the countertop. "That's why I want you to make it with me so you'll get the hang of it. Next we add two-and-a-half cups of flour, or thereabouts."

"It's very simple."

"The simpler the better. Trying to be too fancy with recipes is what gets you into trouble every time."

Angela laughed. "That's so true. It's happened to me more than once." She paused before softly saying, "I used to cook with my mother all the time."

"I'm sure she lived for those times, dear." Mabel patted her shoulder comfortingly.

"I know I did." Angela forced herself out of her sad memory. "I'm sorry."

"For what?" Mabel hugged her shoulders. "I know I'm a poor substitute, but you're welcome to cook with me anytime I'm in town."

"I see why Cam turned out so great." Angela impulsively returned Mabel's hug.

"His father and I had our hands full with that one, but thank the Lord he did turn out pretty well—but don't tell him I said so." Mabel winked. Angela grinned and nodded in agreement. "When his dad passed six years ago, he knew we had raised a great son."

"You certainly did." Angela placed a hand on Mabel's arm. "I'm sorry for your loss."

"Thank you, dear. We had a great life together, and I don't regret a second of it. The good times get me through the pain of losing him." Mabel touched her shoulder. "That's what I want for Cameron—to find a good woman to share his life and start a family with."

Angela didn't respond; she didn't have to. It was clear Mabel thought she was the woman for her son, and what was more disturbing was the fact that despite her resolve to remain emotionally unattached, Angela was beginning to think so, too.

"I think that's mixed enough." Mabel interrupted her introspection, took the bowl, poured its contents into a greased Bundt pan and plopped it into the oven. "Now, we'll let that bake at three hundred twenty-five degrees for about an hour and fifteen minutes."

"Thank you for showing me how to make it."

"It was my pleasure." Mabel kissed her cheek, warming Angela's heart.

"What are my two favorite ladies up to?" Cam drifted into the kitchen like a breath of fresh air.

"Are you finished with your concert?"

Cam chuckled at his mother's question and glanced at Angela. "Angela likes my singing."

"I told Mabel I think you have a great voice," Angela chimed in.

"See." Cam grinned, placing an arm around Angela's waist.

"I think she's prejudiced in your favor, son."

"I hope so." Cam kissed her briefly, but long enough to cause Angela's heart to skip a few beats. "While I was performing, what were you two doing in here?"

"Cooking and getting to know each other," Mabel said.

"Uh-oh, should I be concerned?"

"Now why would you be concerned, Cameron?" Mabel placed a hand on her hip, expression indignant.

"Everything is fine." Angela saved him from answering. "Mabel was showing me how to make a cake."

"Mom, not your pound cake?" Cam's eyes lit up expectantly.

"You know it."

"Angela, wait until you taste it." Cam rolled his eyes in appreciation. "A thousand calories a slice, but so worth it."

"Lord knows I don't need the calories, but nothing's going to keep me from that cake."

"I hope I can live up to all the hype." Mabel laughed.

"You've never disappointed before." Cam kissed his mother's cheek and then turned to Angela. "Are you done in here?"

"Go ahead, dear. I'll be right out once I finish the potato salad."

"Okay." Angela took Cam's hand and walked into the back yard.

"You two looked cozy."

"Your mother's great. She reminds me of happy times with my mom." She tried to keep the melancholia out of her voice, but she wasn't successful because Cam stopped walking as they exited the patio and stared into her eyes.

"Hey, are you okay?"

"I'm fine." She glanced over his shoulder. "Derrick is motioning to you."

"Are you sure you're okay?" At her nod and smile, he kissed her lips lightly before joining Derrick at the grill. Angela walked over to sit beside Alesha, who had moved closer to the grill to sit at a wooden picnic table and bench shaded by a huge umbrella.

"How's everything in the kitchen?"

"Great. Mabel's making a decadent-looking cake."

"We're in for a treat. She can really cook." Alesha fingered Angela's short bangs. "I love your haircut."

"Thanks. Why don't you cut yours? I can give you the name of my beautician."

"Oh, no." Alesha shook her head. "Not if I want to keep my marriage intact."

"It's *your* hair." Angela laughed. "Isn't it?"

"Yes, but I would traumatize Derrick if I cut it. He loves to play with it, and he says there's nothing like the feel of it sliding across his naked body."

"Alesha!"

"What?" Alesha glanced at Derrick and smiled suggestively. "You'd be amazed at the things I can do with my hair that drive him wild."

"Where is my shy little friend?" Angela wondered aloud.

"She married a sexy, virile man who opened up a world of possibilities to her." Alesha winked.

"So I see."

"What about Cam?" Alesha's smile widened when Angela choked on her soda.

"What about him?" Angela set her drink down on the table.

"Does he measure up in bed?"

"I wouldn't know." Angela glanced around, praying no one was listening to their uncomfortable conversation. Cam and Derrick seemed engrossed in tending to the grill, and Mabel was still in the house.

"Please, Angie." Alesha gave her a knowing look. "Don't even try to deny you've slept with him."

"I'm not going to discuss this with you—especially not here." She gave her friend a stern look.

"No one's paying any attention to us," Alesha admonished. "Come on, I'm your best friend, and I seem to recall your being very curious about Derrick and me."

"Okay." Angie sighed in surrender and whispered, "He's very capable. Satisfied?"

"The question is, does he satisfy you?"

Angela's eyes widened, and Alesha laughed. "Alesha!"

"So despite your denials, things *are* serious between you two?"

"We're just…"

"Friends?"

"With benefits." Angela winced at how cheesy that sounded, and Alesha's raised eyebrow informed her she wasn't buying it, either.

"I think you're deluding yourself, but if you say so." Alesha adjusted the volume on the baby monitor.

"I do," Angela firmly reiterated. "I don't want to get serious, and we're just friends." At Alesha's knowing smile, she was compelled to add, "We are!"

Alesha remained silent. Angela sensed her friend knew there was no need for her to say anything further. Angela might not *want* to get serious, but despite her best efforts, she knew it was already much too late to prevent that from happening.

The barbecue broke up early that evening because Mabel had to be at the airport to catch her flight out. Cam and Angela drove her to National Airport and waited until the boarding call for her flight sounded.

"It's been a pleasure meeting you, Angela," Mabel said.

"You, too, Mabel."

"Cam, I expect you to bring Angela for a visit soon."

"Yes, ma'am."

"Well, I guess it's time for me to board." At the second call for her flight, Mabel stood, hugged and kissed them both. "I expect to see you both soon." At the gate, she turned, smiled and added, "Maybe you'll have some good news to share."

"Oh, Mom." Cam chuckled and waved her off. After she disappeared up the ramp, Cam grabbed Angela's hand as they walked away. "That's my mom."

"She's a treasure."

"Thanks." He released her hand and placed an arm around her shoulders. "She liked you."

"I like her, too."

"That's important to me."

"Why?"

He smiled but didn't answer her. There was no need to. "How about going back to my place for some dessert?"

"I'd love to." She had to go back to his place anyway to drop him off, since they had taken her car to the airport, but in her heart she knew she was going with him because she wasn't ready to say goodbye to him yet. She wondered if she would ever be ready for that distasteful prospect.

When they arrived back at Cam's place, they decided to skip dessert in lieu of some intimate alone time in his bedroom. After a satisfying feast of each other, they snuggled together in bed, listening to jazz, occasionally kissing and caressing.

Angela's face was snuggled into the crook of his neck, her open mouth taking love bites out of his flesh, and Cam was in heaven. His fingers ran through her hair and pressed her mouth tighter against his humming flesh. She fit in his life and his world, and he wanted her to always be right where she was—in his arms.

"As good as this feels, babe, I think we need to talk."

"About?" Her voice was muffled against his skin.

"Us."

She tensed in his arms and was silent for several deafening seconds before responding. "Do you *really* want to talk right now?"

"Yes." He forced her mouth away from his neck and glanced into her carefully guarded eyes. "Let's talk about our relationship."

"Are you sure that's what you want?" She nipped at his jaw and promised, "I'll bet I could make you change your mind."

"Could you now?" Despite his desire to talk seriously, he smiled when she crawled on top of him and provocatively slid her satiny body against his hard one. "You think so?"

"Mmm-hmm." She smiled confidently. "I can make you forget everything except loving me in just three easy steps."

"Oh, this I have to see."

A perfectly arched eyebrow rose. "Is that a dare?"

"It is."

"Okay." She scooted down his body until her lips were level with his smooth, muscled chest. "Here's one."

Her hot, wet mouth opened over his nipples, nipping, tugging and laving each bud with her capricious tongue, scraping his disks with her strong teeth until they became hard and distended. When satisfied with the results, her mouth moved down his stomach, where the muscles contracted under her targeted manipulations. Her tongue delved in and out of his belly button before trailing wet kisses across his lower abdomen.

He groaned, and she removed her lips from his tasty skin to smile up into his tense face. He raised his head, and his eyes opened and met her confident gaze.

"How am I doing?" she whispered.

"Keep going," he ordered hoarsely.

"My pleasure." Her hard nails trailed up his sides before moving to the front, working their way down his chest, scraping his nipples and lower abdomen. "That's two."

"Uh-huh." He ground his head into the pillow as she moved even lower. His skin was on fire.

"And this." Her hands moved up and down his hard outer and inner thighs, followed by her mouth. "This is three."

Her mouth attached to him with wet, hot suction, and she mercilessly treated him to heaven, sucking hard and twirling her tongue around and around his rigid flesh. He hissed in approval before breathless groans vibrated from his constricted throat. His body squirmed as Angela refused to stop her sweet torture, even when his hands moved to the back of her head, trying to pry her away from his overstimulated flesh. Finally, after endless licks, sucks and nibbles, she released him and crawled back up his body until her smiling lips were inches from his.

"Do you still want to talk?"

"No!"

She smiled cattily and gasped when he rolled her beneath him.

"I win," she proclaimed smugly.

"We both do," he hoarsely corrected her, crushing her mouth with his for long moments in a voracious kiss. His hands were shaking so badly he couldn't put the condom on, so she took it from him and did the honors, almost sending him over the edge with her slow, tortuous movements. "You've pushed me too far." His voice was raspy with desire.

"I sincerely hope so," she purred as he nestled intimately against her.

Without another word, he plunged into her. She arched up to meet him. She scratched his back, he bit her shoulder; they were ferocious and neither apologized. Because of Angela's previous ministrations, when the moment of gratification came, Cam went over first. When he moved a hand between their bodies and massaged her aching clit, Angela quickly followed him into madness.

Chapter 13

Lying in Cam's strong arms felt like heaven to Angela. She wanted to stay right where she was, and she intended to do just that. Carefully tilting her head, she stared at Cam's closed eyes and relaxed face. He was so handsome, and he was hers. Her fingers froze before making contact with his face. Her fingers trembled slightly as her heart slammed against her ribs.

Is that how she thought of Cam—as hers? Her heart arrested as she realized it was. Part of her was happy about that fact, and part of her was apprehensive. She liked her life the way it was, uncomplicated, career oriented. She loved not having to please anyone but herself—or at least, she had until Cam had so easily insinuated himself into every nook and cranny of her life. She hadn't meant for this to happen, but it had. Now what was she going to do about it?

The vibration of her phone drew her attention away from Cam's relaxed face and roused her from her disturbing thoughts. She snatched the instrument from the nightstand, groaning when she recognized the phone number on the display.

"Hello?" she whispered, trying not to wake Cam. She listened and responded, "Okay, I'll be there as soon as I can." Sighing, she replaced her phone on the nightstand and turned to face a wide-awake Cam.

"Who was that?" Cam sleepily asked.

"The hospital."

"Oh, no," he groaned.

"I know. I'm so sorry." She bent down and kissed him, got out of bed, stepped into her sundress and stated the obvious. "I have to go."

Cam pulled back the covers and sprang out of bed in his naked glory. "Can't someone else handle this?"

"I'm the head nurse," she reminded him. "One of the surgeons whose O.R. team I'm on has an emergency surgery, and he wants me there. It's my responsibility. I have to be there."

"Of course you do." He frowned, bent down, picked up his pants and stepped into them.

She sported a frown of her own. "What is that supposed to mean?"

He sighed and ran a hand over his face. "Nothing."

"No, it's not nothing." She regarded him with a raised eyebrow and informed him, "My career is just as important to me as yours is to you."

"I know it is."

"Do you?" Her eyes narrowed and she challenged, "Then why are you acting like it's not?"

"That's not what I meant to imply. I just wish…" He tried to find the right words to de-escalate what was quickly evolving into an unnecessary argument.

"What?" She zipped her dress up as far as she could and presented her back to him. He quickly pulled the zipper up and then dropped his hands from her instead of pulling her close as he normally would have done. "Spill it, Cam."

He sighed heavily and stated, "There's nothing to

spill." He took one of her hands in his. "I'm sorry if I sounded jealous of your career. I'm not."

She studied his expression and realized he really wasn't jealous, but he was also still upset. "You're not?"

"No." He gave her a slight smile. "Come on, I'll walk you out." He waited for her to don her shoes and pick up the remainder of her belongings before following her out.

"Cam…" She paused at the front door, unsure of what to say.

"Look, I'm not angry, okay?"

She studied his seemingly calm face with skepticism. "I don't believe you."

"I'm not." He took her hands in his. "I'm just disappointed that our night is being cut short." Before she could interject, he continued, "I understand it's your job, but I don't want you to leave. For once, I'd like to wake up with you in my arms."

"I don't want to leave, either," she stated truthfully. "But I have to."

"I know." He opened the door and then turned to face her again. "We have to sit down and talk about what we both expect and need from this relationship, Angela."

She sighed heavily. "Why do you feel the need to complicate things?"

"I'm not trying to—quite the opposite, in fact." He paused as if trying to choose his words carefully. "We're more than friends, Angela—much more." Determined eyes stared into hers. "I think we both realize that, and we need to talk about what comes next."

She ran fingers through her bangs. "I can't deal with this now."

"You're going to have to sooner rather than later."

Her shoulders stiffened at his softly delivered ultimatum. "Good night, Cam."

"Good night."

They stared at each other for several tense seconds before she broke eye contact and walked toward her car. She knew he was right. She couldn't expect him to live in limbo with her, but she didn't know if she was ready to completely let him into her heart, thus risking the devastation that would follow if they couldn't make a go of it.

She started the ignition and exited the driveway. She shook her head to clear her jumbled thoughts. She needed her wits about her. She'd think about what she was going to do about her relationship with Cam tomorrow.

Cam swiveled in his chair and stared out the glass wall of his office at the beautiful view of downtown Washington. Grabbing his phone from the desk, he dialed Angela's number and waited impatiently for her to answer.

"Hello?"

"Hi, babe. How are you?"

"Hi, Cam. I'm good, how are you?"

"I'm good. I'm sorry about last night."

"You already apologized," she softly reminded him.

"I know, but I want to assure you that I do know how important your career is to you, that I support you wholeheartedly and that I wouldn't change a thing about you."

"You wouldn't?"

"No, you're perfect the way you are."

"Well, I don't know about that." She laughed.

"Well, I do," he insisted. "Listen, are you free for dinner tonight?"

"Yes, I am."

"Good. I'll pick you up at seven. Is that good?"

"That's great. How should I dress?"

"To kill."

"Mmm." She chuckled. "Where are we going?"

"It's a surprise." It was going to be a surprise in more ways than one. He couldn't wait to see her face tonight once he asked her what he was going to. He had decided he needed to show her how he felt about her. He didn't think anyone had ever taken the time to show her how special she was, and he intended to remedy that travesty tonight.

"Okay, I like your surprises."

"Good. I'll see you tonight."

"Yes, you will," she promised. "Bye."

"Bye, babe."

He smiled and replaced his phone on the desktop. Tonight was going to be a new beginning for both of them. He couldn't wait to show Angela that he wanted her in his life permanently.

Cam watched Angela while her eyes slowly took in their opulent surroundings in one of the ritziest restaurants in town before returning her awestruck gaze on him. He held out her chair for her before sitting down across from her. Everything was as he had ordered. He smiled when she fingered the red roses in the table centerpiece.

"Did you rent out the entire floor?"

"I did," he admitted with a chuckle when her eyes widened in shock.

"Cam," she gasped. "You shouldn't have."

"Oh, yes, I should have," he quickly countered, taking her hand and squeezing her fingers lightly. "I wanted you to know how sorry I am for last night, Angela."

"Will you stop apologizing?" she chastised.

"Eventually." He winked.

They dined on lobster and steak with baby potatoes and spring vegetables. Everything was cooked to perfection, and dessert was a decadent chocolate cake drenched in chocolate sauce and whipped cream.

"Oh, my Lord, I'm stuffed!" Angela sat back in her chair with a groan, and Cam laughed.

"Good, that means you're too weak to resist what I have in store for you next." Angela smiled at his mischievous grin.

"And what might that be?" When he continued staring at her without responding, she asked self-consciously, "What? Do I have something on my face?"

"No." He shook his head and took a small black velvet box out of his jacket pocket and handed it to her. "This is for you."

"Wh—what is that?" With wide eyes, she glanced at the small box lying in her palm before lifting apprehensive eyes to his sparkling ones again.

"Open it—" he grinned and rubbed his hands together in anticipation "—and find out."

"Cam…" She made no move to open the box, but rather set it down on the table as if she was afraid of what it contained.

"Aren't you going to see what's inside?"

"You didn't have to buy me anything." She lightly fingered the box. Nervousness poured off her in waves, and he covered her hand in his, squeezing reassuringly.

"I didn't spend any money on this." He motioned to the box and laughed at her confused expression. "It's nothing sinister or expensive."

"Promise?" She slowly picked up the box again.

"Yes, I promise." He grinned expectantly. "Open it."

She released his hand, untied the white bow and carefully raised the lid, revealing a brass key. She picked it up and glanced at him in confusion. "What is this?"

"The key to my house." He took her free hand in his

and asked, "Move in with me, Angela." She gasped and dropped the key as if it burned her.

"What?" she whispered.

"I said move in with me," Cam repeated, bringing her hand to his lips.

"Well?" he prodded when she remained silent.

"Cam…" She picked up her glass and took a gulp of her water. "I—I can't."

His smile disappeared. "Why not?" he asked quietly.

"Because you're moving too fast."

"I don't think I am." He caressed her cheek with his thumb. "Angela, we're good together and I know you feel the passion and the *rightness* between us. I want you with me, and I think you want to be with me, too."

"I…" She swallowed hard. She looked terrified, which was the last thing he wanted. "I don't know what to say."

"Look, I know you've had some bad experiences with men. They didn't deserve you." He squeezed her hand reassuringly and promised, "All I want is the chance to make you happy."

"You can't handle my career," Angela blurted out, the first criticism that popped into her head. "Do you think it's going to get any better if we move in together?"

"That's not true, Angela."

"Isn't it? Last night—"

"I've apologized about last night," he quietly reminded her.

"Yes, you did, but what happens the next time my job interferes with our plans?" She stared at him. "And it will interfere."

"I'll deal with it."

"The way you did last night?" He had the feeling she was deliberately trying to pick a fight, and he wasn't going to accommodate her.

"You're not being fair."

"Fair?" Her eyes widened as she stared at him. "I suppose it's fair for you to spring something like this on me without any warning."

He frowned at her accusation. "I wasn't trying to *spring* anything on you or make you uncomfortable."

"Then what?"

"I wanted to surprise you—to show you how much I care about you." He asked, "Are you so jaded that you can't recognize when someone's trying to be genuine with you?"

"I didn't expect this." She took a deep breath. "It's just too much."

He stared at her long and hard before responding, "Me telling you I care about you and want you in my life long term is too much? Unbelievable."

"What do you want from me?" She lifted her hands in a frustrated plea.

"Do you really want to know?" Without waiting for a response, he succinctly spelled it out for her. "I want you to admit that what's between us is not casual or temporary. I want us to start building a life together, and most of all, I want you to admit to yourself and to me *exactly* what I mean to you, Angela, and I'll be happy to reciprocate."

"Why do you have to complicate things?"

"Why do you have to cling to the delusion that we're just *casual* friends?" he shot back tightly.

"Because we are." She fidgeted under his intense stare. "Look, Cam, I told you from the get-go that I wasn't looking for a serious relationship. I like my life the way it is, and I'm not going to apologize for wanting to keep it that way."

There was a lot he could have said, a lot he wanted to

say. Instead, he stood suddenly and placed his napkin on the table. "I'll take you home."

She opened her mouth to speak but quickly shut it again. He pulled back her chair, and she stood and walked toward the door. He fought the urge to topple the table over and followed her out instead.

This wasn't the way he'd expected the evening to end. He had thought if he *showed* her how much she meant to him, how serious he was about her, she'd realize he was different from the men who had hurt her and reciprocate his feelings. She just wouldn't let her guard down.

Dammit! He was beginning to wonder if he'd ever have what he wanted more than anything—Angela saying she was ready to share his life, forever.

Cam nodded as Derrick walked unannounced into his downtown law office for their weekly lunch date. He returned his attention to the electronic devices on his desk. He typed something on his laptop before picking up his phone when it vibrated, frowning at the screen.

"Don't you ever relax?"

"I am relaxing." Cam glanced up and grinned. "Give me a sec." Cam turned his attention to his phone and sighed heavily. "This new client is so irritating."

"You know you thrive on challenges." Derrick laughed as he sat down.

"True." Cam glanced at Derrick again before returning his attention to his computer. "But believe me, I have enough challenges in my personal life presently to keep me more than busy."

"How are you?" Derrick asked, leaning forward in his chair.

"I'm good." Cam set his phone down after reading a text message and started typing on his laptop again.

"You don't look it." Cam sighed at Derrick's observation. "You look tense."

"Thanks, Mom." Cam glanced up briefly to smirk at him and then went back to typing.

"How are things with you and Angie?"

Derrick's question caused a tightening of Cam's shoulders and had his fingers hovering, unmoving over the keyboard.

"A little frustrating," Cam eventually admitted, then closed his laptop and winced at the decisive click, which bore evidence to the force he had unintentionally exhibited.

"Really? You two looked so cozy at the barbecue. That was only a few days ago. What happened?"

"It's not important." Cam shook his head, took out a bottle of water from the minifridge behind his desk and tossed it to Derrick. "Forget it."

"You really expect that to happen?" Cam smiled at Derrick's determined expression. "Spit it out, Cameron."

"I want Angela to stop pretending that we're just friends," Cam admitted with a loud sigh. "Satisfied?"

"And she won't do that?"

"No." Cam rubbed his neck. "I understand she's gun-shy about relationships, I really do, but I thought by now she'd be ready to at least admit that I matter to her."

"Because she matters to you?"

"Yeah." Cam took a swig of his water. "I don't know. Maybe she doesn't feel the same."

"I don't believe that." Derrick sat forward in his chair. "Anyone looking at the two of you together knows there's something there."

Cam reclined back in his chair. "I asked her to move in with me."

"What?" Derrick's eyes widened.

"You heard me." Cam managed a chuckle at his friend's shocked expression.

"Well, what happened?" Derrick prodded, and Cam's half smile fell.

"She turned me down."

"Damn. I'm sorry." Derrick paused before offering, "Maybe she just needs a little time to get used to the idea."

"What she needs is to stop being scared and take a chance on us," Cam countered, frustration seeping from his pores.

"And she won't?"

"No." Cam sighed. "Her past has made her scared of entrusting her heart to someone, and as much as I try to convince her that we would be different from her past relationships, she just won't believe it. Dammit, doesn't that woman know that I…" A look of complete shock spread across Cam's face.

"What's wrong?" Derrick smiled broadly. "Just realizing that you're in love with Angela?"

Cam blinked at his friend's statement. "How do you know I'm in love with her?"

"I'm your best friend, and I saw it at her birthday party—the way you spoke about her, looked at her. It was written all over your face."

"Yeah, then why doesn't Angela see it?"

"Maybe she does," Derrick suggested. "Maybe that's what's frightening her so much." Cam's brows furrowed as he contemplated Derrick's observation.

"You think?"

"You'd know better than me, although you can be pretty dense sometimes."

"Thanks." Cam shot him a dirty look.

"Just stating a well-known fact, Counselor." Derrick smiled at Cam's scowl.

"Any other words of wisdom you'd care to impart?" Cam crossed his arms over his chest.

"Yes, keep trying to get through to your lady because we both know she's the one for you."

"I have been trying, Derrick," Cam stated, frustration lacing his words. "I'm beginning to think I'm fighting a losing battle."

"Bull!" Derrick's smile disappeared, and he smacked his hand on Cam's desk. "Try some more."

"I'm tired, Derrick. I don't know what else I can do."

"Dammit, Cam, for one thing, you can stop feeling sorry for yourself!"

Cam's eyes widened in surprise, and he sputtered, "I beg your pardon."

"You heard me." Derrick stood, placed both hands on Cam's desk and continued in the same harsh tone. "You've never given up on anything in your life!"

"No, I haven't, but—"

"Well, now is not the time to start—not when we're talking about the woman you love!" He straightened, but continued his stern lecture. "Stop this pity party, pick yourself back up and go fight for her, no matter how much she frustrates you!"

"You're such a hothead." Cam laughed at his friend's scowling face. "You're also very bossy."

"It comes in handy when dealing with you." Derrick lowered his voice and smiled. "Not that I have to ask, but what do you want, Cam, really?"

"I want what you and Alesha have—though you two fought against it like crazy."

Derrick grinned at Cam's pointed reminder. "But if I

remember, a nosy friend kept telling me we should give our marriage a try—make it real."

Cam tilted his head to one side. "I wonder who that was."

"As much as it pains me to admit this, you were right, and now I'm giving you the same advice—make things work with Angela. Don't give up on her, because you know she's *the one*."

"She is it for me, but I can't do it alone, buddy."

"Anything worth having is worth fighting for."

"My, you've gotten philosophical," Cam snorted.

"And wiser. Now, are you going to fight for your lady, or do I have to kick your butt?"

"In your dreams." Cam chuckled, then his eyes lit up with new determination. "Thanks for the pep talk, pal. I needed it."

"Anytime." Derrick seemed rather pleased with himself, and Cam couldn't help grinning. "It's nice to be able to give you unsolicited advice for once."

"Don't let it go to your head. I'm still the wiser one here."

"If it makes you feel better to believe that, go ahead." Derrick chuckled. "Come on, let's go get some lunch." Cam stood, and Derrick patted his back "By the way, you're buying."

"Still cheap, I see." Cam shook his head at Derrick as they walked out of the office, chuckling.

Chapter 14

Angela sat across the table from Alesha and tried to pretend she was happy. She missed Cam. They hadn't spoken or seen each other in a week. She felt lost without him.

"What's wrong, Angie? You seem to be in a funk."

"Nothing. I... Work has just been crazy lately."

"Mmm, I'm sure it has been," Alesha agreed. "But I don't think that's what's bothering you."

"Nothing's bothering me."

"Is it Cam? Are you unsettled by his feelings for you—or yours for him?" Bingo! Alesha hadn't lost her intuitive touch. "Talk to me."

"He wants more than I'm able to give." Angela sighed heavily and admitted, "He asked me to move in with him."

"That's great." Alesha studied her friend's sad face and asked, "Isn't it?"

"I like Cam," Angela slowly said.

"But?" Alesha prompted.

"But I don't know if I want the hassles that come along with trying to navigate a serious relationship."

Alesha cocked a thoughtful eyebrow. "What have you two been doing if not building a relationship?"

"We've been having a good time."

"That's all?"

Angela fidgeted as Alesha treated her to a piercing stare. "Why does there have to be more?" She raked fingers through her hair in frustration. "We have a great time together. Why can't we just keep things casual and avoid the messy complications that come with trying to bite off more than we can chew?"

"Do you really think keeping things as they are is going to satisfy Cam?" Alesha paused and pointedly added, "Or yourself?"

"I just don't need or want any complications in my life right now. Plus, I don't know if he can really handle the demands of my career."

"Why do you say that?"

"He gets upset when the hospital calls and interrupts our plans."

"That just means that he cares and wants to spend time with you."

"I guess, but I'm not going to give up my career for him or any man."

"Has he asked you to?"

"No," she admitted.

"Then stop borrowing trouble," Alesha suggested.

"It's all moot anyway." Angela sipped her coffee.

"Why?"

"Because I have no intention of moving in with him or letting him believe he controls me in any way," Angela said stubbornly.

"I don't think Cam wants to control you, and I think you know that," Alesha replied. "Bottom line, you're terrified of opening your heart to someone. It's no secret that I think you two are great together, but if you really don't see yourself with Cam long term, then tell him so. Cut him loose, let him go on with his life, and you go on with yours without him."

Angela held back a gasp of shock at Alesha's stern suggestion. That was the last thing she had expected her to say, but she was right, and Angela knew it. It wasn't fair to Cam to keep him in limbo because she was afraid to fully commit to him.

She finally knew what she had to do. Why, then, instead of feeling relieved, did she feel sad and empty?

Angela's eyes widened when she pulled into her driveway after work. Cam was leaning against his car waiting for her. She parked the car and took several deep breaths; she was a mass of nerves. Releasing her breath noisily, she slowly got out of her car and walked up to him.

"Hi." She stared at him uneasily.

"Hey." He gave her a half smile but made no move to touch her. "Can we talk?"

"Sure." She motioned to the house, walked ahead of him and unlocked the door. They walked into the living room. "Can I get you something to drink?"

"No. You can sit down with me." He held out a hand to her, which she slowly walked over and took, and they sat on the sofa. "Angela, I've tried to take things slowly with you, no pressure, just letting you get used to having me around."

"I am used to that." He squeezed her fingers and smiled at her soft admission.

"I know, and it scares you, doesn't it?"

"Yes." She took a deep breath, released it and said something completely unplanned. "I've spent so much time closing myself off to avoid being hurt again. It's safer to be alone, and I'd gotten used to it, even liked it, but then you and I started dating and…now, I don't know anymore. I think maybe…" Her voice trailed off, unsure of where she was going with this.

"Maybe what?"

"Honestly, I don't know." She shrugged helplessly.

"What do you want, Angela?" When she remained silent he continued, "Do you really want to stop seeing me? Because if you do, tell me so and I'll walk away for good." Her eyes grew big at his statement.

"You will?"

"Yes, if that's what you want." He stared into her eyes, and she couldn't hide the truth from him if she wanted to. "Is it?"

"Cam…" She closed her eyes briefly, and when she opened her mouth again, the truth tumbled out. "No, I don't want to stop seeing you, but I don't know if I can give you what you want or need." She sighed heavily. "And then there's my career."

"First of all, Angela, I'm not jealous of your career." He held up a hand to stay her and continued, "Yes, there are going to be times when your job interferes with our plans, and my job will do the same. I won't lie to you, I'll hate those times, but I know we can make this work if we both want it enough—if we both try. Will you try?"

"I…" She stared at him helplessly, unsure how to respond.

"Babe, I know you're wary of trusting a man again." His voice was kind and understanding. "You've been hurt by some first-class idiots, but I will never hurt you like that." He stared deeply into her confused, scared eyes. "We can have something terrific—something that only comes along once in a lifetime—if you take a chance on us."

She shrugged, vulnerability present in her eyes. "What if I don't know how?"

"It's easy." He gave her one of his signature smiles.

"All you have to do is take a deep breath, hold on to my hand, and I promise I won't ever let you fall again."

"What if I let you fall?"

"I'm pretty resilient at picking myself up, dusting off and moving forward," he promised. "Ask anybody who knows me." At her baffled expression, he asked gently, "What's wrong?"

"Where's the anger?"

He laughed out loud at her question and brought her hand to his lips before placing her palm against his cheek.

"When I refused to move in with you, I know you were hurt and annoyed."

"I was disappointed. I haven't called you because I was giving you some time to think while I planned my next move."

"You can have any woman you want, Cam." She searched his eyes and asked, "Why me?"

"Because you're it for me, Angela," he responded without missing a beat. "When I look at you, I see a beautiful, fantastic woman who makes me feel like I finally know why I was placed on this earth." He tenderly touched her cheek. "You're authentic, you don't pretend to be flawlessly perfect and you have a heart too kind for this world. I have an amazing time with you, and when we're apart, it's like a piece of me is missing." His words brought tears to her eyes. "I see *everything* in you."

"Cam—"

"No, don't say anything." He brought her hand to his lips again. "We'll finish this conversation when I get back."

A frown marred her face at his unexpected words. "Back from where?"

"I have to go to Atlanta on business for a few days, maybe a week."

"For your new client?"

"Yeah." He sighed audibly as if he wasn't too happy about the trip but was resigned to it nevertheless. "They need a little hand-holding from the boss."

"Are you going to see your mom while you're in town?"

"If I don't at least stop by and say hi, she'll have my head." He chuckled, and she joined him.

"Say hello for me."

"If I do, those matchmaking wheels in her head will really start turning—more than they are already," he warned.

"Say hello for me anyway."

He gave her one of his dimpled grins. "Now you're giving me hope."

"You already had hope." She stared into his confident eyes and laughed when he winked at her. "When are you leaving?"

"Tonight—" He glanced at his watch. "In about three hours, actually. I just found out about it today."

"I'll miss you." His fingers tightened in hers at her easy admission.

"I'll miss you, too, but this separation will be good for us."

"How so?"

"It'll give you time to think without any distractions and decide what you really want."

Her heart thudded at his words. Could she commit to forever? "It'll give you time, too."

He smiled at her tenderly. "I don't need any time, Angela. I already know what I want—you." He placed a hand behind her neck, pulled her close and kissed her thoroughly. "When I come back, we'll talk again and see what you've decided."

"What if I haven't made a decision by then?" His eyes clouded over a little at her question.

"As much as I want you in my life…" He paused, and she could tell his next words were difficult for him to utter. "I don't intend to live in limbo with you indefinitely."

"Meaning?"

"Meaning when I get back, either we start making plans for our future or we end it. It's your choice, babe." She didn't want the fate of their relationship in her hands, but she guessed it had always been that way.

"I'm afraid," she whispered.

"I know, but you don't have to be with me." His tender smile melted her heart and almost made her believe him. "I want you to have faith in that." He stood and pulled her to her feet. Hand in hand, they walked to the door. "I'll see you in a week. Promise me you'll think while I'm gone."

"I promise."

"In a week, we move forward together." He sounded so certain. She wished she could be. He kissed her, and she held on to his strong shoulders and sank into the kiss, never wanting to let him go. When they broke apart, she felt bereft. As if sensing her mood, he promised, "I'll see you soon."

"Bye, Cam. Be safe." He smiled at her and kissed her again, much too briefly.

"Miss me," he ordered before leaving.

She missed him the second the door closed behind him. Damn, that man always said and did the right things. She'd never met anyone like him. More than anything, she wanted to take a chance on him—on them—but could she open completely up, lay her wary heart bare and let go of her past demons to do that? She had been on her own for so long; it was safe and comfortable. It was also lonely.

Could she willingly take a leap of faith and place her heart and soul in someone else's hands? That was the million-dollar question.

The next couple of days dragged by. Angela wasn't fit to be around—a fact her coworkers soon realized. They steered far away from her unless absolutely necessary.

She sat in her office going over the nurses' schedule without really seeing it. She was preoccupied and unhappy. Everywhere she looked, she saw Cam's smiling face. Sighing heavily, she threw her pen down onto the desk, swiveled in her chair and stared out the window at the beautiful day with a deep frown marring her face.

Cam had only been gone for two days, and she had worn herself ragged thinking about him and them. She felt as if she were climbing the walls. She missed him that much.

She was accomplished in her professional life. No one would dare call her timid or incompetent when it came to treating patients, so why was she allowing herself to be such a frightened rabbit in her personal life? Cam had done something no one ever had for her—he'd committed to a future with her, and all he wanted in return was for her to give him a chance to make her happy. He *did* make her happy—happier than she'd ever been in her life.

She had a wonderful man, and she was about to lose him because she was terrified of what *might* happen down the road in their relationship, when the truth was that no one could predict the future. Cam was right. It was way past time that she took a chance, and by God, that's what she was going to do!

Swiveling in her chair to face her desk, she came to a

long-overdue decision. Picking up her phone, she began making calls to clear her schedule for the next week.

Cam opened the door to his suite, and his eyes widened in pleased shock at the sight of Angela staring at him, smiling. God, he had missed her beautiful face, her soft musical voice and the incredible feel of her in his arms.

"Hi, Cam."

"Angela, what a great surprise." Cam took her hand and pulled her inside.

"Wow, this is some room." She glanced around the huge suite, then propped her roll-away suitcase against the door and moved closer to him. "Very nice."

"You know I like to be comfortable." His arms snaked around her waist. "Why didn't you tell me you were coming?"

"You're always surprising me. This time I wanted to surprise you." She placed her hands around his neck. "How about a proper welcome?"

"Anything you say, ma'am." He slowly, painstakingly lowered his mouth to hers, watching her eyes the entire time. When their lips finally touched, both groaned and dove in without hesitation. They acted as if they hadn't seen each other in years instead of only days. They kissed as if they would never stop. When their mouths reluctantly parted, both were breathless. "How was that?"

"Great for starters," she whispered, pulling his mouth back to hers.

"Not that I'm complaining," he murmured against her lips long seconds later. "But why are you here, babe?"

"I missed you." The look in her eyes communicated how true that simple yet important statement was, and he knew that which he had waited so patiently for was about to materialize. "So much."

"I missed you, too." He pulled her to the sitting area, and they sat closely on the sofa. "Did you think while we were apart?"

"Yes." She ran a hand down his cheek as if she couldn't bear to not touch him. "A lot."

"Make any decisions?" He captured her hand and briefly brought it to his lips.

"Some major ones." She seemed more at peace than he had ever seen her, which sent hope soaring through him.

"Well?" His eyes teased. "Are you going to let me in on them?"

"Yes, I'm just trying to decide where to start." She took a deep breath and released it before beginning, "You asked me to judge you for you and not by anyone else's standards, and I'm ready to do that."

He smiled brightly at her words, and her fingers traced his lower lip softly. "You are?"

"Yes." She nodded. "From day one, you've been wonderful to me—I didn't expect it, and I certainly wasn't used to it. I just couldn't believe you were for real." She paused and kissed him softly before continuing, "As time went on, I realized you were very sincere in your feelings for me."

"I am," he confirmed.

"I know, but I wasn't used to that. My experience with men has consisted of being hurt, and I was determined not to let that happen again, so I tried to keep things controlled and manageable." She shook her head, sighed, caressed his face with her fingers and continued, "And then there was my career. I've worked so hard to get where I am, and I honestly liked my life the way it was before we started dating—predictable, comfortable and uncomplicated. The only person I had to worry about or please was me, and the thought of suddenly having to consider someone else terrified me. It still does, but I've finally come to terms with the one important fact." She paused. "I can no longer imagine my life without you in it.

"Good." He grinned, and she smiled. "Now, tell me the rest of it."

She gasped and asked, "How do you know there's more?"

"I sensed it." His thumb made soothing circles on her cheek. "I knew you'd tell me when you were ready."

"I'm ready now." She took a deep breath and released it before she spoke of the greatest pain in her life. "When I was fourteen, my dad left me and my mother. Out of the blue one day, he just packed up and left. He sent my mom a letter stating he was leaving her for someone else, and later came the divorce papers."

"Damn, that's cold."

"It was horrible." She closed her eyes briefly at the awful memory. "There were no warning signs. I thought we were happy." She paused and then forcefully corrected herself. "No, I *know* we were. He and I were very close. He taught me about sports, took me to the big games. To this day, I don't understand how he left without saying a word to me. He never wrote or called."

"I'm sorry, baby. He was wrong for that." She remained silent, lost in the painful memories, and he gently asked, "Did you ever see him again?"

"No. The fact that he didn't want to communicate with me hurt for a long time." She paused before admitting, "I guess it still does hurt."

He held her close for a few seconds and then pulled back to stare into her sad face. "I can find him for you if you'd like."

"No. Thank you for offering, but if he wanted to see me, he would have found me."

"I understand." He ran soothing hands down her arms. "I just want you to know that I'm here for you. Whatever you need, all you have to do is ask and it's yours."

"You are so special." Love shone from her eyes as she looked at him, and he couldn't wait for her to say the three little yet monumental words he had waited so long to hear her confess—but first things first.

"Finish it," Cam said gently, knowing she wasn't done yet.

"Okay." He didn't think it was possible, but her eyes grew sadder. "After my dad left and it became apparent he wasn't coming back, I watched Mom enter into one disastrous relationship after another. The men she dated weren't interested in long-term or happily ever after. When she had enough of searching for that ever-elusive, unconditional love she sought, she turned to booze to dull the pain, and once she dove into that bottle, she never came out again." Cam listened raptly, his heart breaking for the pain Angela had endured. No wonder she didn't have faith in relationships. "She held it together enough to keep a job, a roof over our heads, and I never wanted for anything materially, but I had to sit helplessly by while she drank herself to death over my father. I guess I've always been afraid I'd end up just like her—a lonely old woman who, for reasons beyond her comprehension, lost the only man she ever loved and spent the rest of her life slowly dying from a broken heart." She sighed heavily and concluded, "Lord knows, the few relationships I've had have mimicked hers."

"Until now." Cam placed a hand under her chin and forced her eyes to meet his. "You're definitely long-term relationship material."

"I think maybe I am with you."

"Believe it, baby," Cam urged. "You are a wonderful person, Angela, and I'm so glad you're in my life."

Her fingers tightened in his, and she confessed, "I still…"

"Go on, babe. Tell me."

She took a deep breath and released it. "I'm still afraid we won't last."

"We will. Do you want to know why?" At her nod he continued. "Because we're meant to be. I'm not interested in a fling. I want a commitment from you—a *lifelong* commitment, and I want it now. I want to go to bed with you by my side and wake up with you there. I want to come home and sit with you on the sofa and talk about our day. I want to cuddle with you in front of the TV and fall asleep that way. I want to build a family with you." He watched her closely as she digested his carefully worded and delivered desires. "No more delays, and no more excuses. It's time for us to start our lives together. How do you feel about that?"

"I'm yours, Cam." He framed her face with his palms and kissed her lingeringly before pulling back slightly. "I have been from the second I laid eyes on you."

"You're everything to me, Angela." He stared deeply into her eyes so that she could see the validity of his statement. "You infuse my gray world with brilliant color."

"I'm so blessed you want to share your life with me."

"You're not going to get an argument from me on that." She playfully punched him in the stomach, and they laughed until she sobered. "I'm terrified that this happiness I feel won't last."

"There are no guarantees in life, babe." He paused. "Except one."

"What's that?"

"I'll love you for as long as I live."

"That's good enough for me." She stared deeply into his eyes and finally allowed herself to confess, "I love you, too, Cam. I've never loved anyone like this." A brilliant smile lit up his eyes at her words.

"I've waited a long time to hear you say that."

"I know, and now that I have, I'll never stop admitting it." She ran her hands over his beautiful bald head and kissed him until they both groaned. "I'll always love you, Cam."

"I'll always love you, too, babe." Her heart overflowed with happiness at his sincerity.

"I didn't want to fall in love with you, but I couldn't help it."

He grinned. "So you're saying I'm irresistible?"

She laughed, and her fingers caressed his cheeks. "At the risk of feeding your already enlarged ego, yes, you are completely irresistible."

He cocked an eyebrow. "What do you mean enlarged ego?"

She chuckled. "Shut up and kiss me, Cameron."

"I can do that."

"Nobody does it better," she said softly, and his smile lit up the room.

Chapter 15

Their lips gravitated together and touched. Cam's mouth played with hers in butterfly caresses until she thought she would go mad. He nipped at her lower lip before soothing it with his tongue, which only served to make her want him even more. She cradled the back of his head in her hands and tried unsuccessfully to pull his mouth down to hers.

"What do you want, baby?"

"I want you." She groaned the words against his lips, and he smiled.

"You've got me," he promised before taking her mouth in a heated, thorough kiss.

Angela's eyes slid closed, and without hesitation, her mouth opened wide beneath the coaxing pressure of his. They should have been incinerated on the spot by the depth of their passion for each other. Tongues twined and dueled, lips pressed and caressed and hearts beat only for each other as they greedily fed from each other's mouths like famine victims.

Despite the fact that she was completely breathless from their sweltering kisses, she protested when he lifted his mouth from hers. Opening dazed eyes, she was nearly blinded by the scorching heat, desire and, most of all, the love overflowing from him as he smiled at her.

"How long can you stay?"

She stared unblinkingly into his eyes and promised, "Forever."

"Good answer." He rewarded her with another satisfying kiss. "But I meant how long will you be in town?"

"Oh." She laughed softly. "I took the week off."

"That *might* be enough time for me to begin showing you how much I love you." He stood and pulled her to her feet before enfolding her in a tight embrace. "I've got one last meeting tomorrow, but after that, I'm all yours. We can take a minivacation."

"What about tonight?" Her mouth playfully sparred with his. "Are we done talking, I hope?"

"Oh yeah." He effortlessly scooped her up into his arms and carried her into the bedroom. "We are definitely done talking—with words anyway."

They removed each other's clothes with a frenzy borne out of pure desire and absolute love—wanting and needing to show and feel how much they meant to each other. Angela lay on the bed and purred when Cam followed her down, his hard body pinning hers to the mattress. Not a word was spoken verbally, but their hearts silently proclaimed their true and undying love loudly, perfectly and reverently.

Angela gasped against Cam's warm lips when her body effortlessly conformed to his as if she had been made solely for that purpose. She trembled uncontrollably from the overwhelming rapture that engulfed her entire heart, body and soul as Cam's body breached hers. There was nothing like the wonderful feeling of him coming home where he belonged.

How had she ever lived without him? She honestly didn't know, but she was so thankful she would never be alone again. Cam would always be with her, and she would forever stand by his side. They occupied and would continue to occupy places in each other's hearts that nothing and no one could ever violate or destroy.

Angela arched against Cam's hardness, wrapping her legs around his waist, pressing and pulling closer to his muscled strength that she needed to survive. She wanted to be absorbed by him, completely and utterly forged into his one true and perfect mate. They couldn't get close enough, deep enough into each other, but oh, how they tried to defy the laws of physics and achieve the impossible—creating oneness out of two.

This time their lovemaking was familiar and yet different—made more special by the fact that Angela didn't hold any part of herself back. She freely gave her heart and soul to the man who had taught her all about unconditional true love.

Their echoing groans and sighs of rapture filled the room with the sweetest music the world had ever known as she gave everything she had to Cam and received all she needed in return.

Early the next morning before sunrise, Cam awoke with a start. Turning his head and simultaneously reaching out his hand to the other side of the bed, he found empty space. Angela wasn't there. Sitting up, he silently chided himself. After their wonderful, perfect reunion last night, she had to be here. Still, he was about to get out of bed to check when she walked into the bedroom smiling, bringing the sunshine in with her.

"Good morning," she happily greeted him. She was wearing one of his T-shirts and had a breakfast tray in her hands. Walking over, she placed the tray on the bedside table before plopping down on the edge of the bed and kissing him soundly, as if she could go on and on forever. "Did you think I was gone?"

"Of course not," he lied, propping back against the pillows.

"You did." She traced his chin with her fingers. "Didn't you?"

"Absolutely not." He gave her his best poker face.

"Right." She laughed and then solemnly promised, "You're stuck with me for life."

"Hallelujah!" He tried to pull her down to him, but she resisted. "What?"

She took a deep breath, released it and said solemnly, "I have something very important to ask you."

"So ask, and then I want a proper good morning from you."

"Deal." She took his hands in hers and asked, "Cameron Stewart, I love you with my whole heart. Will you marry me?" When he remained noticeably silent, she frowned. "Well?"

"I don't know." He retrieved one of his hands from her to thoughtfully rub his chin. "This is all so sudden."

She punched him in the ribs playfully. He laughed and pulled her close, and his mouth made a beeline for hers, capturing her lips for long, satisfying seconds.

"Of course I'll marry you," he answered between kisses. "Just try to stop me."

"You'd better—" she traced his lower lip with her fingers "—because I've spoken to your mother about this."

"You spoke with Mom? When?"

"Yesterday, before I came to see you. We had a wonderful talk, and she really wants a grandbaby." Her face grew thoughtful. "I think she's started planning our wedding already."

"Are you serious?"

"Of course I am." She laughed. "She thinks we're perfect together."

"I can't argue with her there."

"She made me promise to get you to the altar as soon as possible."

"I guess there's only one thing left for me to do, then."

"What's that?"

He brought her hands to his lips before asking, "Angela Brown, for my mother's sake, for my legacy's sake and mostly for my sake, will you marry me?"

"Yes, yes I will." She sealed her promise with a sweet kiss and then pulled back to add, "I can't wait to marry you, Cam."

"That's good because I don't want a long engagement."

"You won't get an argument from me on that." She sealed her statement with a heated kiss.

"After my meeting today, do you want to go shopping for rings?"

"Oh yes!" She threw her arms around his neck and his arms went around her, pulling her until she was lying on top of him. "I love you so much."

"It took you long enough to figure that out," he whispered in her ear.

"Hey." She pulled back to smile at him. "I came around, didn't I?"

"Finally." He groaned the word and then smiled teasingly. "I knew you couldn't resist my formidable charm forever."

"You are so conceited." She shook her head at him in mock reproof.

"Self-assured," he said, nipping at her lower lip playfully before their mouths melded in a passionate kiss. "Mmm, I love your sweet mouth."

"Yeah? Show me how much." She pulled his lips back

down to hers, and they feasted for interminable seconds. "It should be illegal to be this happy."

"It's not." Her fingers caressed his cheek, and the unabated love reflected in her eyes was the most beautiful thing he had ever seen. "You deserve to be happy, babe."

"All I want or need for that to happen is you, Cam." Her arms pulled him down until his body was pressed against hers.

"You've got me." He lowered his mouth toward hers. "Forever."

"Forever." She breathed the promise against his lips.

They sealed their promise with a sweet yet passionate kiss.

After a three-hour meeting, Cam returned to the hotel in the afternoon and changed into jeans and a T-shirt before whisking Angela off to a swanky downtown jeweler to buy her ring. They ate a late lunch and then made their way to Cam's mother's house. Angela glanced at the three-carat diamond solitaire in a platinum setting residing on her finger and smiled happily.

"Do you really like it?" Cam intercepted her glance.

"Are you kidding? I love it." She kissed him briefly. "Though I still think it's too much."

"It's not enough," he contradicted. "I wanted the five-carat one, remember?"

"Please, I'd be terrified to wear it." Angela placed her free hand to her heart. "As it is, I'm going to have to get used to this one."

"You'll get used to it." He kissed her hand.

"I think I will." They drifted together until their mouths met. Simultaneously, they moved closer, arms automatically going around each other, and then they were soon kissing deeply. The screen door opened without either of them realizing it.

"Well, are you two just going to stand there and give the neighbors a peep show, or are you coming in?" They started apart and glanced at Cam's mother, who was smiling widely at them.

"Hi, Mom." Cam grinned and put a hand on Angela's lower back to usher her inside.

"Angela, it's wonderful to see you, dear."

"You, too, Mabel."

"I'm so glad to see you two together and looking so happy." Mabel showed them onto the screened-in deck at the back of the house. "I hope this means…" Her voice trailed off when Angela held up her left hand and showed off her engagement ring. "Hallelujah!" Mabel placed one arm around both and hugged them tight.

"It doesn't take much to make her happy." Cam laughed as he and Angela sat on a wicker sofa with floral cushions. His mother sat across from them in one of the matching chairs.

"Finally, my wayward son is getting married!"

Cam chuckled at his mother's enthusiasm, and Angela joined him.

"There's so much to do! Let's see, we'll have to decide on flowers, music, your dress, of course, and the preacher." Mabel ticked off things to do on her fingers. "You two are having a real wedding and not planning on going to a justice of the peace, aren't you?"

"I want a big wedding," Angela answered, and Mabel nodded in agreement. "I only plan on getting married once, so it has to be right."

"Anything you want, babe." Cam kissed her hand. "The sky's the limit."

"Generous to a fault." Angela kissed his cheek.

As if unable to resist the temptation of the nearness of her mouth, he turned his head and kissed her. As usual when they touched, she melted. It took her several minutes to remember where they were and that Cam's mother was watching them. Thus, she reluctantly pried her lips from his and glanced at Mabel in apology.

"What are you grinning at, Mom?" Cam's question gave Angela a few seconds to compose herself.

"I'm just imagining the beautiful babies you two will make." Mabel's eyes grew wistful. She hastily added, "Once you're married, of course." Cam and Angela laughed.

"Don't worry, Mom, we'll make you some *legitimate* grandbabies." He grinned at Angela, who was too overcome with emotion to speak because the thought of having Cam's baby filled her with joy.

"I can't wait to hold him or her." Mabel smiled wistfully.

"Well, you'll have to wait a little while, unless Angela's been keeping secrets from me," Cam teased.

"Cam!" Angela blushed, and he laughed heartily.

"We're not planning a lengthy engagement, so we can get to work on that grandbaby soon, Mom." He treated Angela to one of his gorgeous smiles, which made up for him embarrassing her. "Right, babe?"

"Right."

"That's wonderful. You'd make a lovely June bride, Angela, but since it's the middle of May, that doesn't leave us much time to plan everything." Mabel's brows furrowed thoughtfully and she added, "That is, of course, if you'd like my input."

"Mabel." Angela reached across and squeezed her hand. "I'd love your help planning the wedding. In fact, I insist."

Mabel smiled brightly at Angela's words. "You know

I'm thrilled to help in any way." She motioned to her son, who was smiling tolerantly at her. "I've been waiting *forever* for this one to settle down."

"I had to find the right woman, didn't I?" Cam reasoned.

"Yes, dear, I know you did." Mabel smiled at Angela. "And, may I say, you picked a winner."

"I know I did." Cam kissed Angela's cheek.

"Thank you both." Angela had never felt so loved. "Mabel, I think between you, me and Alesha, we can get everything planned by the end of June," Angela predicted.

"We'll get it done. They don't call me *the organizer* at church for nothing." Angela laughed at Mabel's proud smile. "Since we'll be family soon, dear, I'd be so happy if you'd call me Mom."

Angela's smile fell. Her voice stuck in her throat. She didn't think this day could get any better, but she had been wrong. She had been so long without a mother, and now to have one... She was overwhelmed with emotion. She felt Cam and Mabel staring at her, concern evident in their eyes, and yet she was unable to speak for a few uncomfortable seconds.

"I'm sorry, dear. I didn't mean to upset—"

"No," Angela whispered, trying to hold back tears. "You didn't upset me. It's just that I never thought..." She fought back tears. "I'd love to call you Mom."

"Then it's settled." Mabel squeezed her hand, and Cam kissed her cheek.

"Mom, before you get bogged down in wedding planning, what's for dinner?"

"Cam, we just ate," Angela reminded him.

"That was a snack." He glanced hopefully at his mother. "Now I'm ready for some home cooking."

Mabel shook her head at him and said to Angela, "This one loves to keep me in the kitchen."

"Can I help it if you're an excellent cook?" Cam grinned. "Besides, if we didn't stay for dinner, I'd never hear the end of it."

"First things first, Cameron. I'll rustle up something filling once we make a dent in these wedding plans," Mabel promised. "Speaking of food, though, I was at the grocery store this morning and just happened to see some bride magazines. I guess a little birdie told me I should buy them."

"Oh really?" Cam shook his head tolerantly. "You just *happened* to see them?"

"Shush, or there'll be no food for you." Mabel shook a stern finger at Cam, who made a zipping motion across his lips. Mabel picked up several magazines from the side table and handed them to Angela. "An outside wedding will be just beautiful this time of the year, but there's nothing like an old-fashioned church wedding, either. Which would you prefer, Angela?"

"Outside sounds perfect," Angela decided as she slowly flipped through a magazine and then glanced at Cam. "Maybe in your backyard?"

"Anywhere you want, babe." Cam picked up her hand and kissed her fingers one by one.

"What kind of flowers would you like for your bouquet?" Mabel asked. "Angela?"

"What?" She shook her head and tried to focus on Mabel's question. "I'm sorry, Mabel." She stared into Cam's mischievous eyes. "I can't concentrate with you touching me like that."

"Really?" He moved closer to her side and scraped his teeth over the tip of her index finger. "Just focus on me then, babe." Angela's breath caught in her throat as tentacles of awareness shot up her spine.

"Cameron, behave," Mabel ordered sternly. "You can be romantic later. Right now, we have a lot of planning to do."

"Yes, ma'am." Cam released Angela's hand but whispered in her ear, "Wait until I get you alone."

Angela fought a groan at his promise and tried to focus on what Mabel was saying instead of the desire rocketing through her as she stared into the hungry, loving depths of her fiancé's eyes.

Fiancé—was there a better word in the English language? She didn't think so. On second thought, *husband* quickly came to her mind. She couldn't wait to be able to call Cam that.

When Cam and Angela arrived back at the hotel later that night, both were happily exhausted. They sat side by side on the sofa. Angela sighed and snuggled close into his side. This had been an absolutely perfect day.

"Happy?"

"Deliriously happy." Angela's contented voice and smile echoed the truth of her words.

"Me, too." Cam hugged her tight. "Mom didn't overwhelm you too much, did she?"

"Not in the least." Angela's smile widened, and she laughed. "She's so excited about the wedding—almost as much as I am."

"She's like a kid in a candy shop," Cam agreed. "Personally, I can't wait for our honeymoon." He glanced down at her when she laid her head on his shoulder. "By the way, can you get time off from the hospital for a real honeymoon? I want to take you somewhere exotic."

"I have over a month of vacation time, so I'm sure it won't be a problem."

"Good."

Angela snuggled into his warm embrace. "I can't believe in a little over a month we'll be married."

"Believe it, because I'm not letting you go, babe."

"I'm not letting you go, either." She placed her palm over his heart. "I hope you're sure I'm what you want."

"You're the one I want, Angela. Always." He kissed her as if he would never stop, and she participated wholeheartedly.

Once they came up for air, Cam stood, pulled her up and scooped her up into his arms, carrying her into the bedroom. Along the way, she made a symphony of kissing his strong jaw and neck. Cam set her down beside the bed and slowly peeled off her clothes, and she delighted in returning the favor in between kisses. Once they were entwined on the bed, the same slow pace continued. They savored each touch, each kiss, each sensation.

Angela pulled Cam's mouth down to hers, and they kissed long and deep. She loved kissing him. She'd be content to spend the night just memorizing every nook and cranny of his pleasure-giving mouth. She never knew that a kiss could send her heart racing feverishly against her ribs, causing her entire body to tingle like a million skillful fingers were stroking her, or nourish her soul the way nothing else in this world could. She realized only a kiss from Cam could fill her up to bursting and give her everything she needed to be happy and fulfilled.

All coherent thoughts fled from her mind as Cam's hands, mouth and body skillfully played her pliant flesh like an accomplished musician mastering his instrument, coaxing the sweetest music from her. Their bodies strained closer and hearts became one as they silently proclaimed their undying love to each other.

Later, lying close, completely at ease and feeling whole for the first time in a long, long time, Angela thrilled at her unshakable, complete happiness.

"You'd better be here when I wake up in the morning." Cam's soft warning disturbed the peaceful quiet.

"I guess you're just going to have to wait and see." She ran her palm down his smooth chest before kissing his pecs lingeringly.

"If you're not—" his hands slowly traveled down her bare back to rest on her hip "—I'm going to hunt you down and bring you back."

"Ooh," she murmured. "Caveman behavior turns me on."

"Really?" His hands wandered over her bare skin with increasing insistence.

"Mmm-hmm." She snuggled closer to his warm, hard body. "But you've completely worn me out for now."

"Okay." He kissed the top of her head. "Rest, babe."

"I love you," she whispered sleepily.

"I love you, too." Strong arms enfolded her, and shortly she fell asleep in his arms, feeling more loved and secure than she ever had.

When Cam awoke the next morning to bright sunlight filtering softly through the windows, a contented smile spread across his face because Angela was still nestled snugly in his arms where she belonged—where he knew she would remain. Forever.

* * * * *

Just in time for the holiday season!

FARRAH ROCHON
TERRA LITTLE
VELVET CARTER

HOT
Christmas
NIGHTS

Fan Favorite Authors
FARRAH ROCHON
TERRA LITTLE
VELVET CARTER

These new novellas offer perfect holiday reading! Travel to Tuscany, Las Vegas and picturesque Bridgehampton with three couples who are about to experience very merry seduction against the perfect backdrops for everlasting love.

Available October 2014 wherever books are sold!

HARLEQUIN®
www.Harlequin.com

KPHCN1601014

The first two
stories in the
Love in the Limelight
series, where four
unstoppable women
find fame, fortune
and ultimately…
true love.

LOVE IN THE LIMELIGHT

New York Times
bestselling author
BRENDA JACKSON
&
A.C. ARTHUR

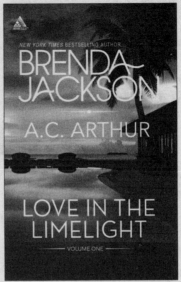

In *Star of His Heart*, Ethan Chambers is Hollywood's most eligible bachelor. But when he meets his costar Rachel Wellesley, he suddenly finds himself thinking twice about staying single.

In *Sing Your Pleasure*, Charlene Quinn has just landed a major contract with L.A.'s hottest record label, working with none other than Akil Hutton. Despite his gruff attitude, she finds herself powerfully attracted to the driven music producer.

Available October 2014 wherever books are sold.

H HARLEQUIN®
™ www.Harlequin.com

REQUEST YOUR FREE BOOKS!

2 FREE NOVELS
PLUS 2 FREE GIFTS!

KIMANI™
ROMANCE

Love's ultimate destination!

KROM13R